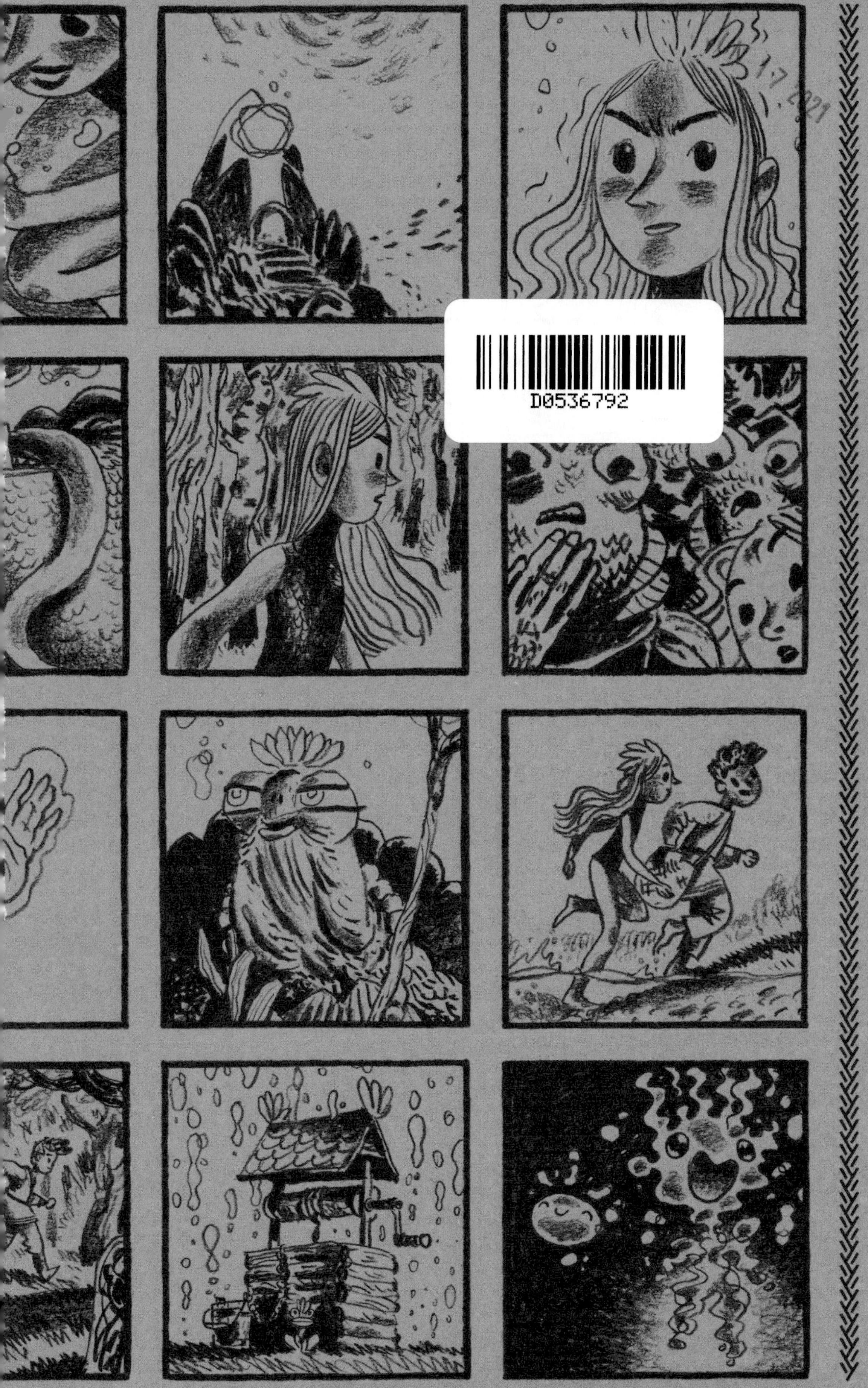

TO LYNA, MY PARENTS, FRIENDS,
HERGÉ & J. R. R. TOLKIEN.
UTKIN

GAMAYUN
TALES

BASED ON RUSSIAN
FOLK TALES

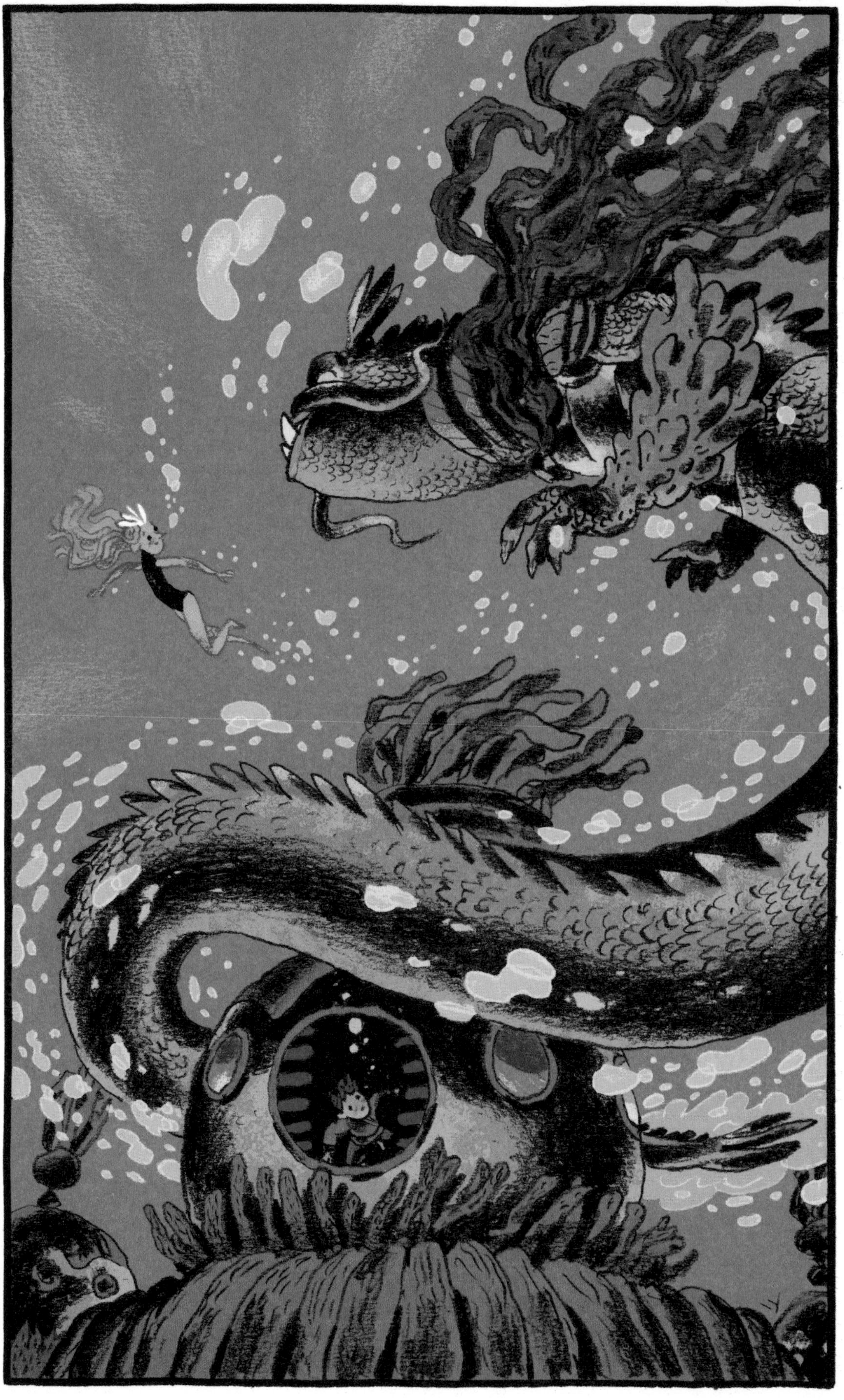

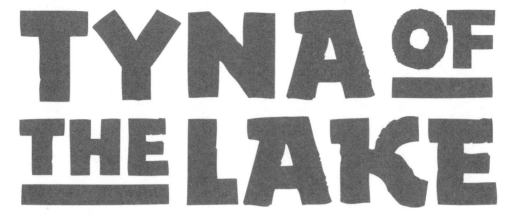

TYNA OF THE LAKE

WRITTEN & DRAWN BY
ALEXANDER UTKIN

TRANSLATED BY
LADA MOROZOVA

NOBROW
LONDON | NEW YORK

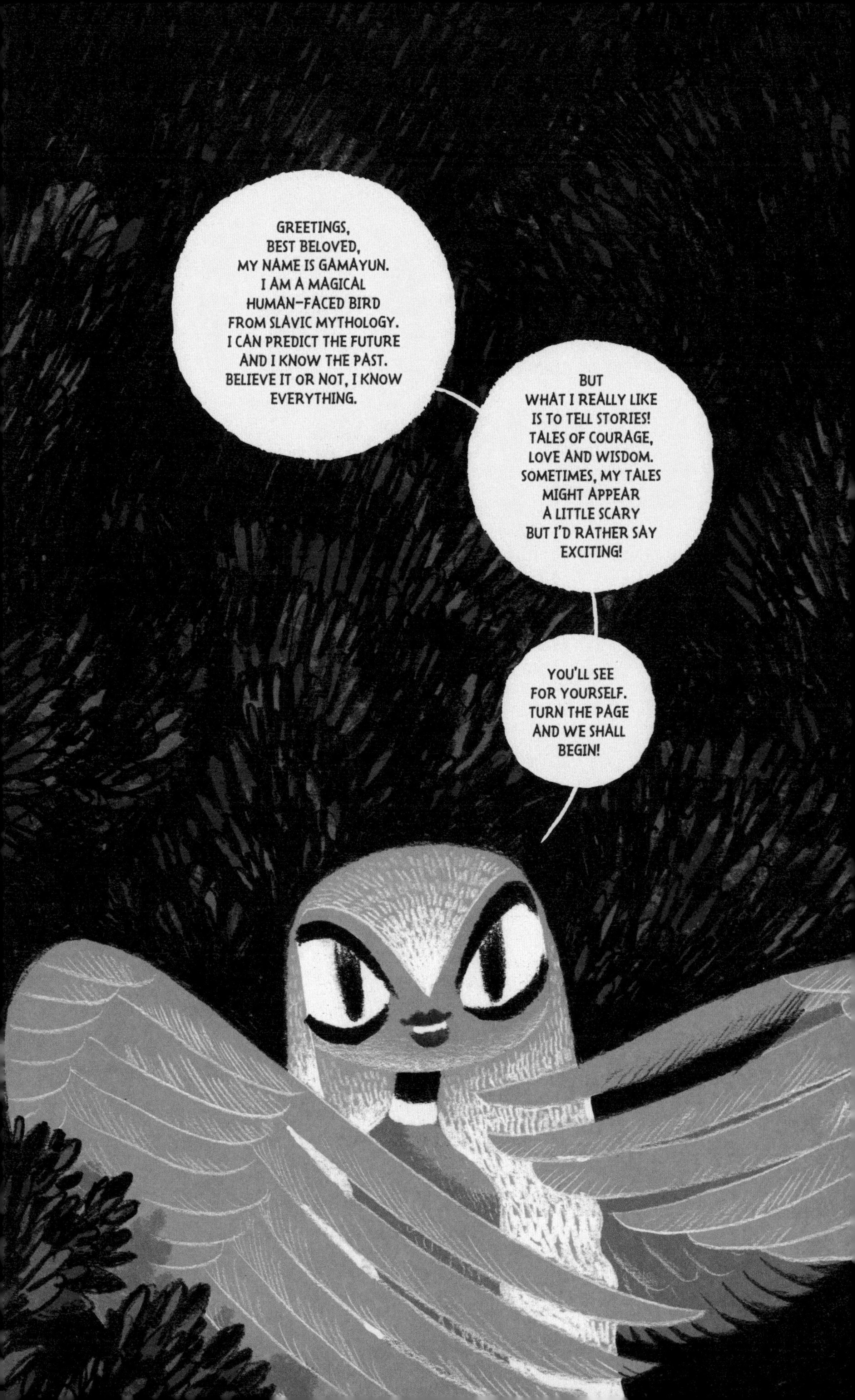
GREETINGS, BEST BELOVED, MY NAME IS GAMAYUN. I AM A MAGICAL HUMAN-FACED BIRD FROM SLAVIC MYTHOLOGY. I CAN PREDICT THE FUTURE AND I KNOW THE PAST. BELIEVE IT OR NOT, I KNOW EVERYTHING.
BUT WHAT I REALLY LIKE IS TO TELL STORIES! TALES OF COURAGE, LOVE AND WISDOM. SOMETIMES, MY TALES MIGHT APPEAR A LITTLE SCARY BUT I'D RATHER SAY EXCITING!
YOU'LL SEE FOR YOURSELF. TURN THE PAGE AND WE SHALL BEGIN!

VODYANOY

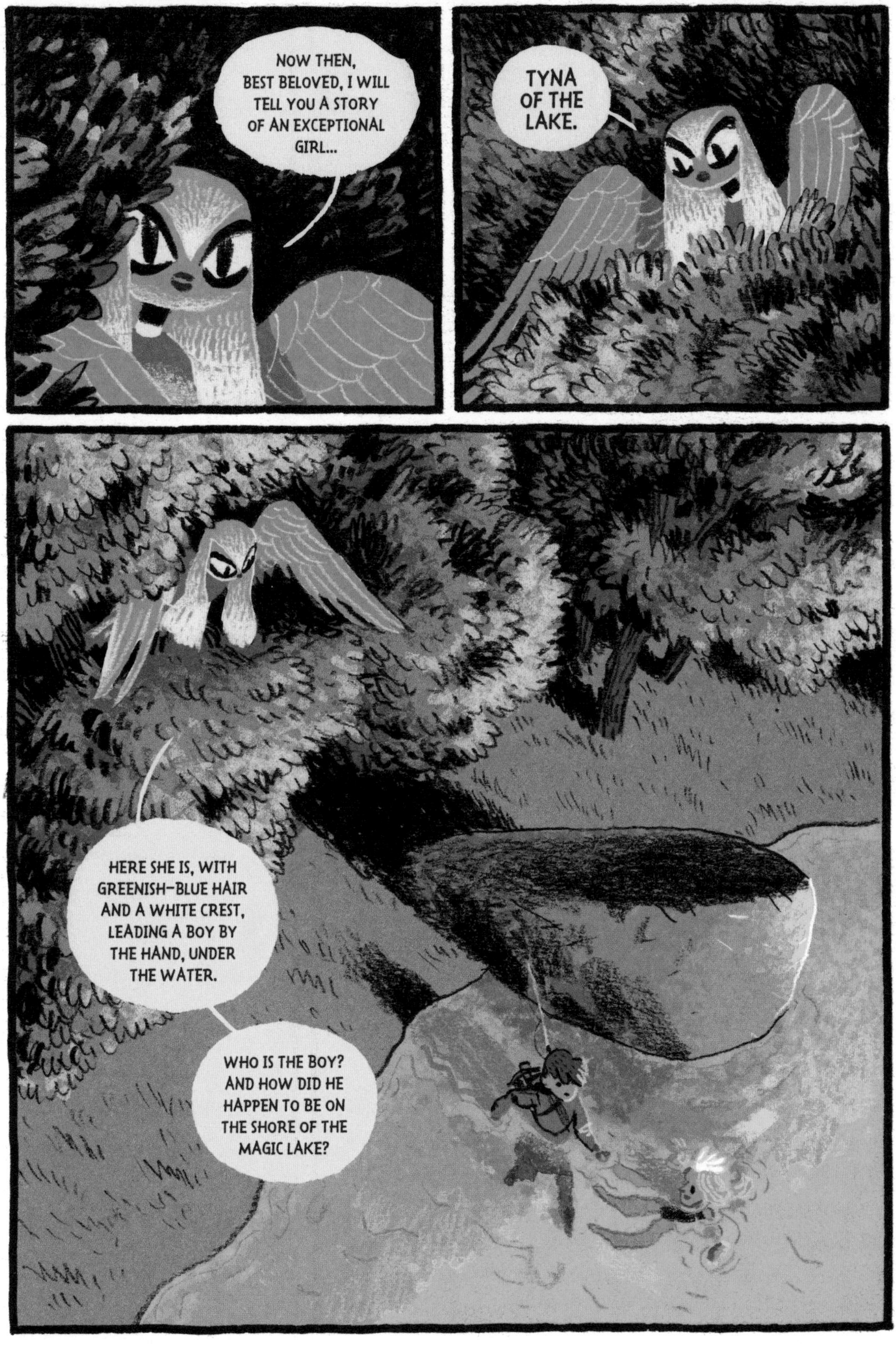
NOW THEN, BEST BELOVED, I WILL TELL YOU A STORY OF AN EXCEPTIONAL GIRL...
TYNA OF THE LAKE.
HERE SHE IS, WITH GREENISH-BLUE HAIR AND A WHITE CREST, LEADING A BOY BY THE HAND, UNDER THE WATER.
WHO IS THE BOY? AND HOW DID HE HAPPEN TO BE ON THE SHORE OF THE MAGIC LAKE?

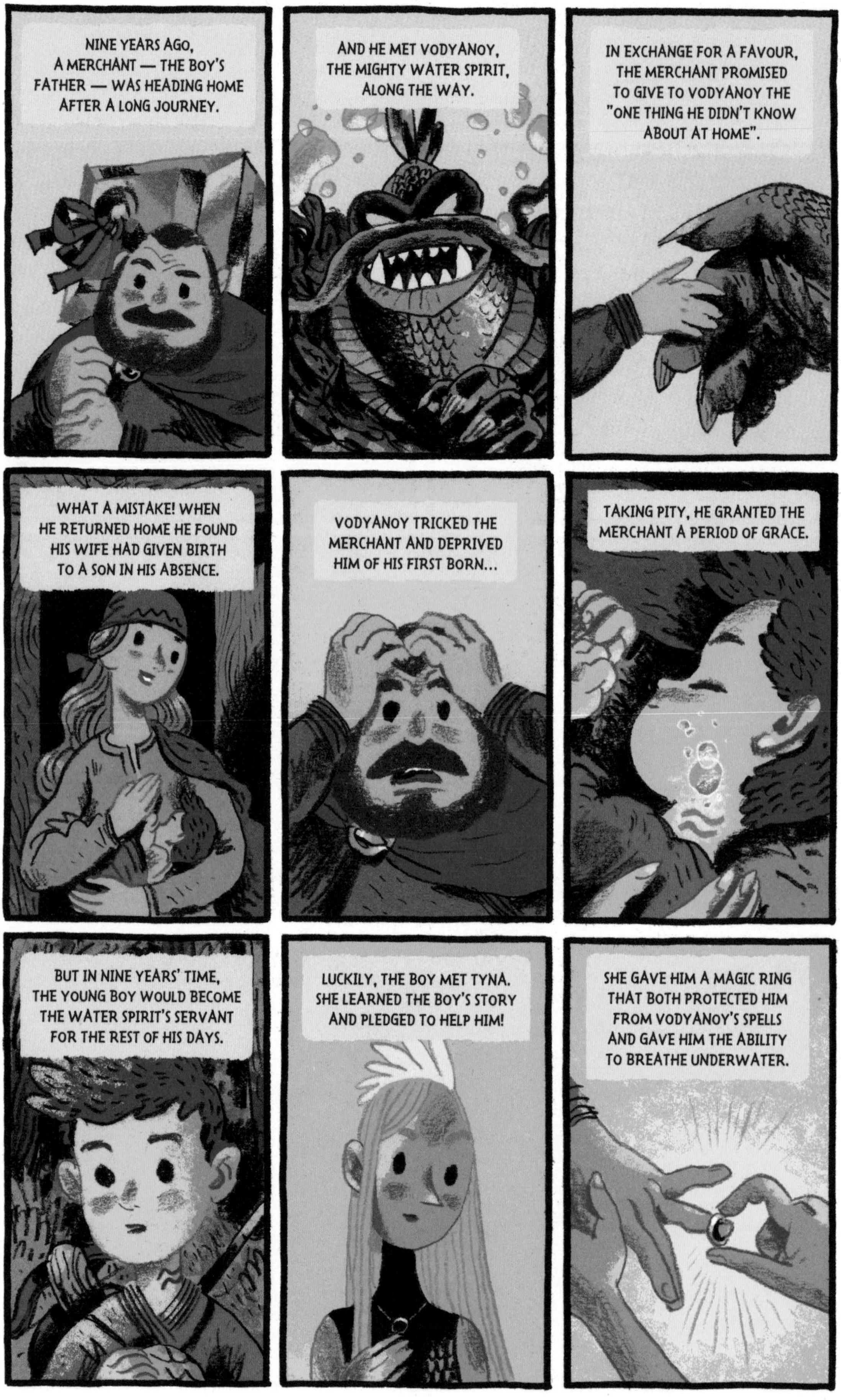
NINE YEARS AGO, A MERCHANT — THE BOY'S FATHER — WAS HEADING HOME AFTER A LONG JOURNEY.
AND HE MET VODYANOY, THE MIGHTY WATER SPIRIT, ALONG THE WAY.
IN EXCHANGE FOR A FAVOUR, THE MERCHANT PROMISED TO GIVE TO VODYANOY THE "ONE THING HE DIDN'T KNOW ABOUT AT HOME".
WHAT A MISTAKE! WHEN HE RETURNED HOME HE FOUND HIS WIFE HAD GIVEN BIRTH TO A SON IN HIS ABSENCE.
VODYANOY TRICKED THE MERCHANT AND DEPRIVED HIM OF HIS FIRST BORN...
TAKING PITY, HE GRANTED THE MERCHANT A PERIOD OF GRACE.
BUT IN NINE YEARS' TIME, THE YOUNG BOY WOULD BECOME THE WATER SPIRIT'S SERVANT FOR THE REST OF HIS DAYS.
LUCKILY, THE BOY MET TYNA. SHE LEARNED THE BOY'S STORY AND PLEDGED TO HELP HIM!
SHE GAVE HIM A MAGIC RING THAT BOTH PROTECTED HIM FROM VODYANOY'S SPELLS AND GAVE HIM THE ABILITY TO BREATHE UNDERWATER.

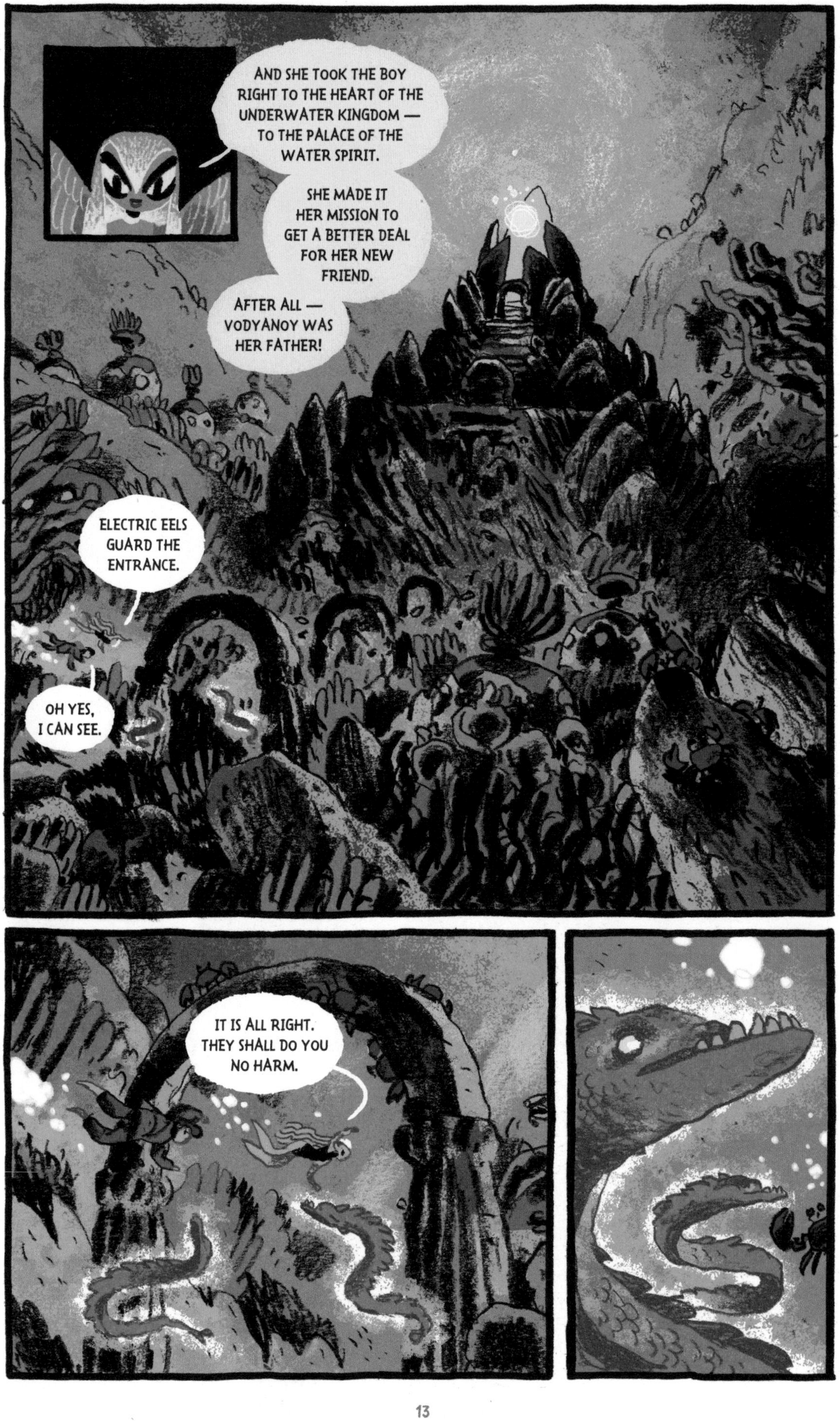
AND SHE TOOK THE BOY RIGHT TO THE HEART OF THE UNDERWATER KINGDOM — TO THE PALACE OF THE WATER SPIRIT.
SHE MADE IT HER MISSION TO GET A BETTER DEAL FOR HER NEW FRIEND.
AFTER ALL — VODYANOY WAS HER FATHER!
ELECTRIC EELS GUARD THE ENTRANCE.
OH YES, I CAN SEE.
IT IS ALL RIGHT. THEY SHALL DO YOU NO HARM.

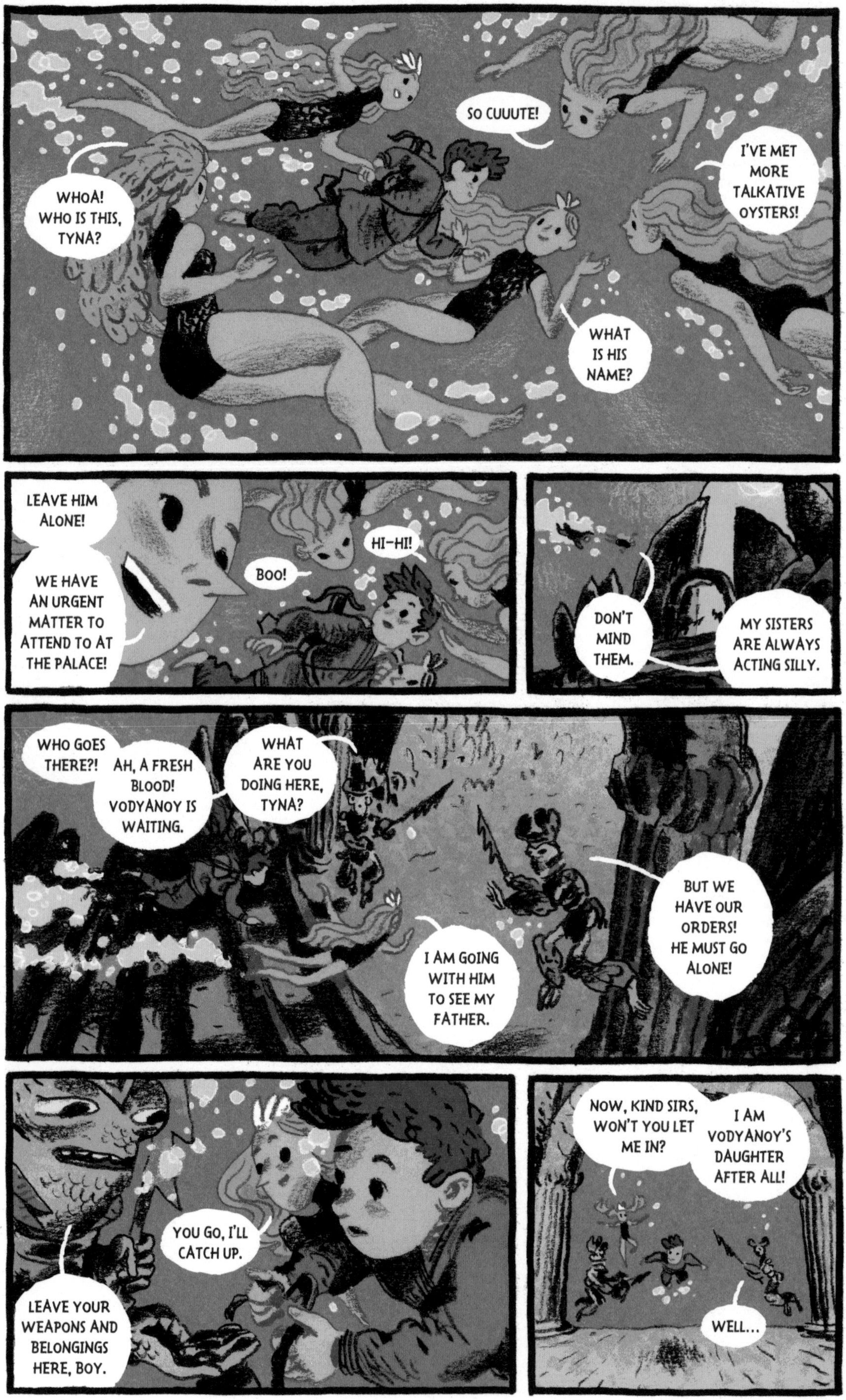
SO CUUUTE!
WHOA! WHO IS THIS, TYNA?
I'VE MET MORE TALKATIVE OYSTERS!
WHAT IS HIS NAME?
LEAVE HIM ALONE!
WE HAVE AN URGENT MATTER TO ATTEND TO AT THE PALACE!
BOO!
HI-HI!
DON'T MIND THEM.
MY SISTERS ARE ALWAYS ACTING SILLY.
WHO GOES THERE?!
AH, A FRESH BLOOD! VODYANOY IS WAITING.
WHAT ARE YOU DOING HERE, TYNA?
I AM GOING WITH HIM TO SEE MY FATHER.
BUT WE HAVE OUR ORDERS! HE MUST GO ALONE!
LEAVE YOUR WEAPONS AND BELONGINGS HERE, BOY.
YOU GO, I'LL CATCH UP.
NOW, KIND SIRS, WON'T YOU LET ME IN?
I AM VODYANOY'S DAUGHTER AFTER ALL!
WELL...

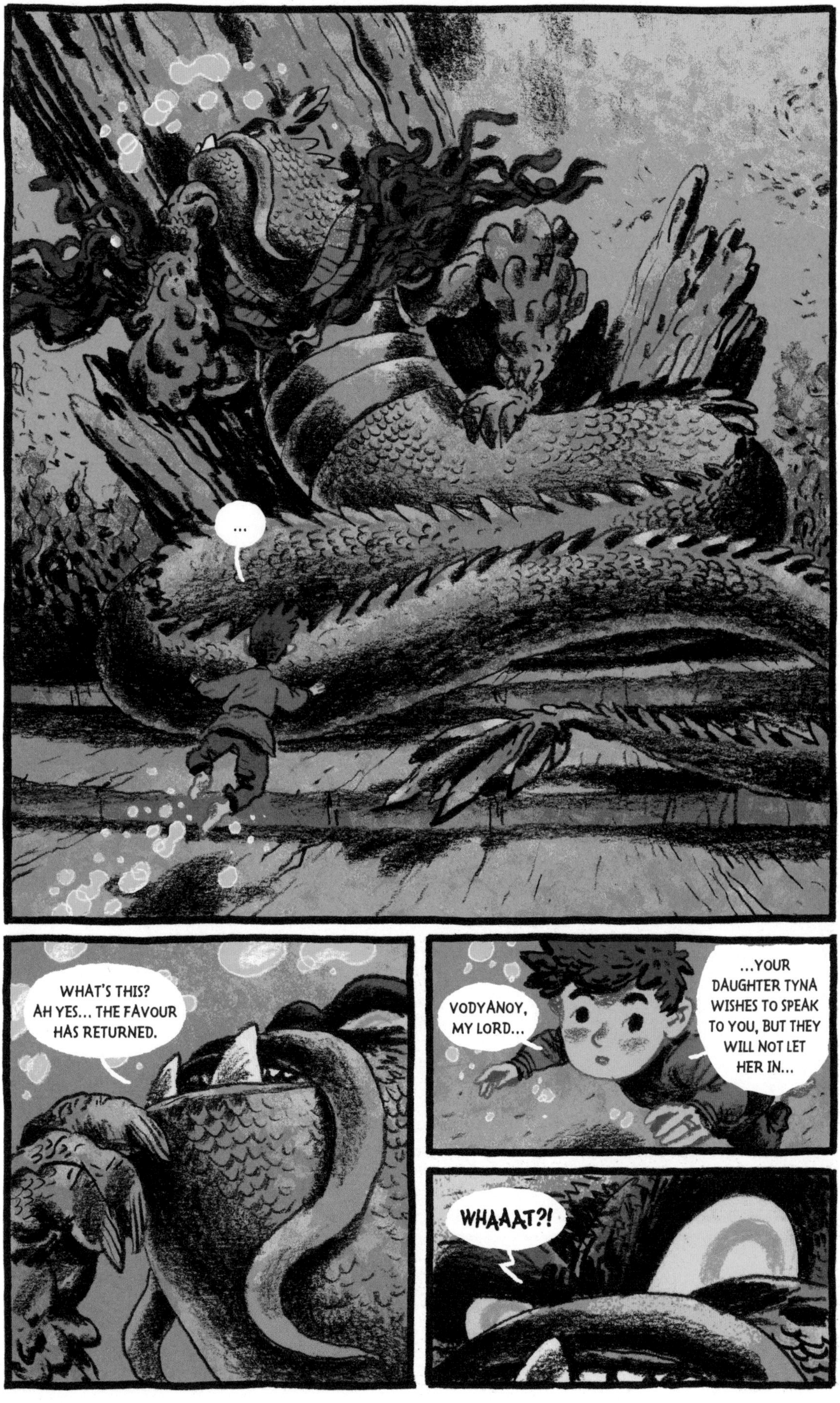
...
WHAT'S THIS? AH YES... THE FAVOUR HAS RETURNED.
VODYANOY, MY LORD...
...YOUR DAUGHTER TYNA WISHES TO SPEAK TO YOU, BUT THEY WILL NOT LET HER IN...
WHAAAT?!

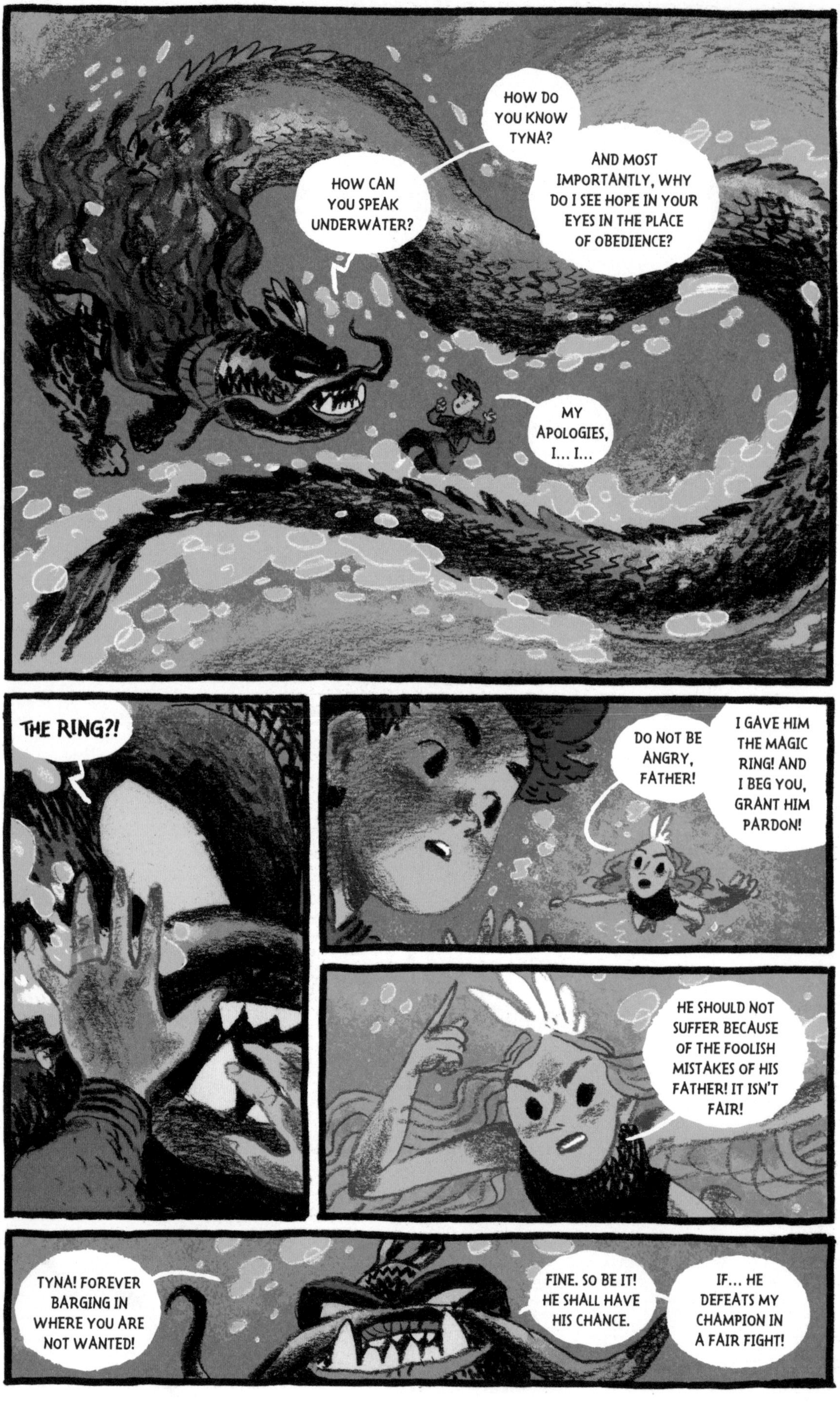
HOW CAN YOU SPEAK UNDERWATER?
HOW DO YOU KNOW TYNA?
AND MOST IMPORTANTLY, WHY DO I SEE HOPE IN YOUR EYES IN THE PLACE OF OBEDIENCE?
MY APOLOGIES, I... I...
THE RING?!
DO NOT BE ANGRY, FATHER!
I GAVE HIM THE MAGIC RING! AND I BEG YOU, GRANT HIM PARDON!
HE SHOULD NOT SUFFER BECAUSE OF THE FOOLISH MISTAKES OF HIS FATHER! IT ISN'T FAIR!
TYNA! FOREVER BARGING IN WHERE YOU ARE NOT WANTED!
FINE. SO BE IT! HE SHALL HAVE HIS CHANCE.
IF... HE DEFEATS MY CHAMPION IN A FAIR FIGHT!

THE FIGHT

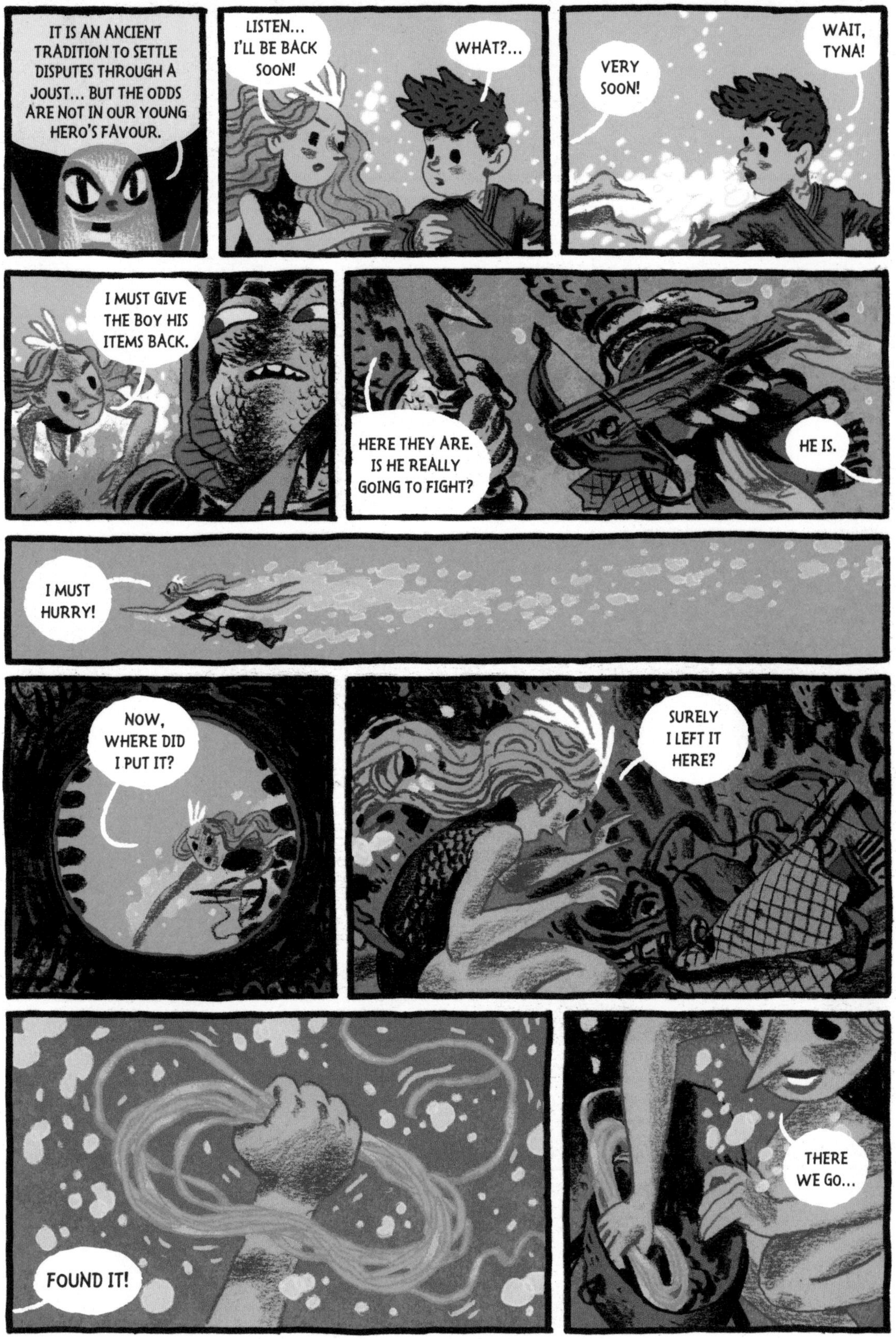
IT IS AN ANCIENT TRADITION TO SETTLE DISPUTES THROUGH A JOUST... BUT THE ODDS ARE NOT IN OUR YOUNG HERO'S FAVOUR.
LISTEN... I'LL BE BACK SOON!
WHAT?...
VERY SOON!
WAIT, TYNA!
I MUST GIVE THE BOY HIS ITEMS BACK.
HERE THEY ARE. IS HE REALLY GOING TO FIGHT?
HE IS.
I MUST HURRY!
NOW, WHERE DID I PUT IT?
SURELY I LEFT IT HERE?
FOUND IT!
THERE WE GO...

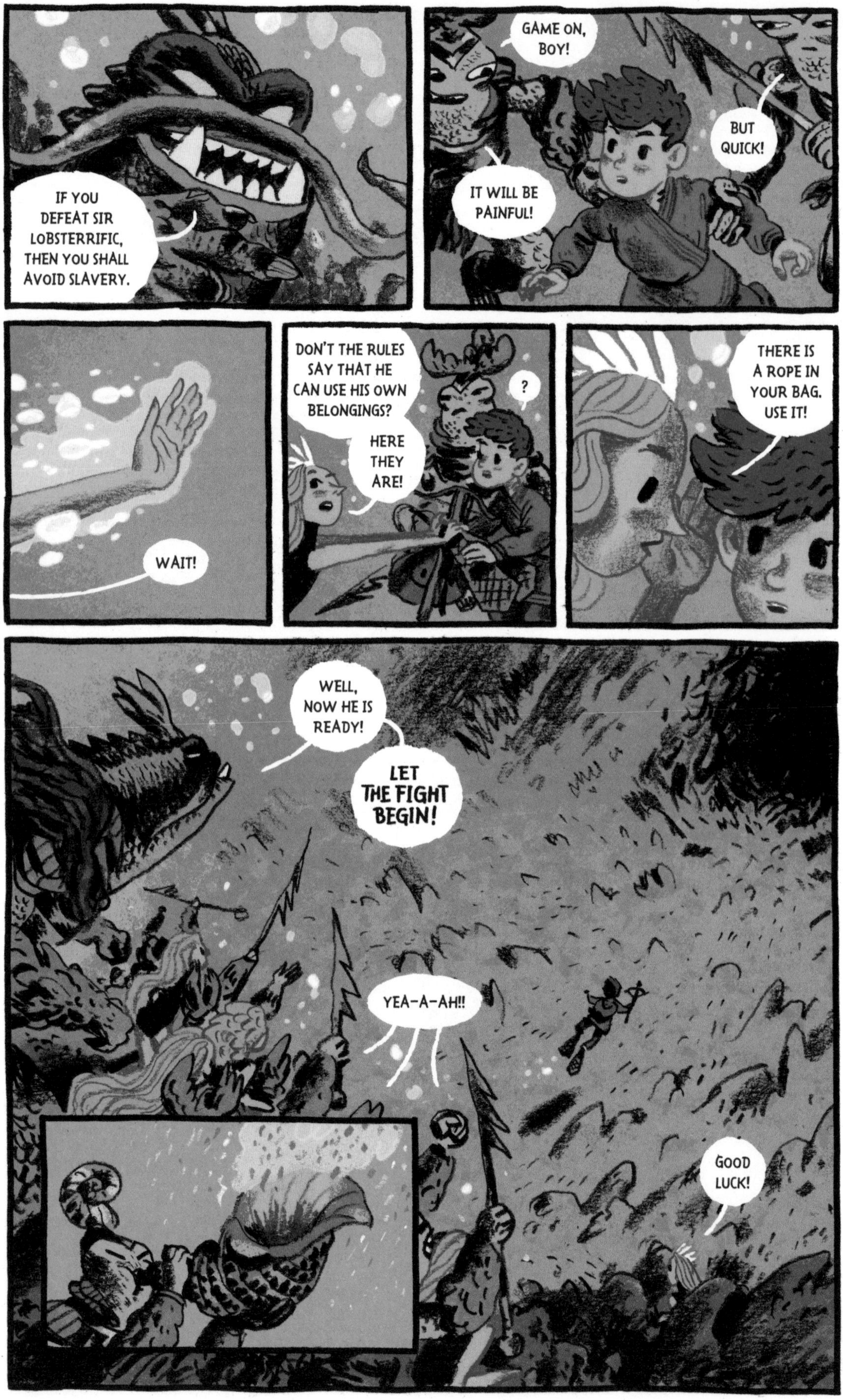
IF YOU DEFEAT SIR LOBSTERRIFIC, THEN YOU SHALL AVOID SLAVERY.
GAME ON, BOY!
IT WILL BE PAINFUL!
BUT QUICK!
WAIT!
DON'T THE RULES SAY THAT HE CAN USE HIS OWN BELONGINGS?
?
HERE THEY ARE!
THERE IS A ROPE IN YOUR BAG. USE IT!
WELL, NOW HE IS READY!
LET THE FIGHT BEGIN!
YEA-A-AH!!
GOOD LUCK!

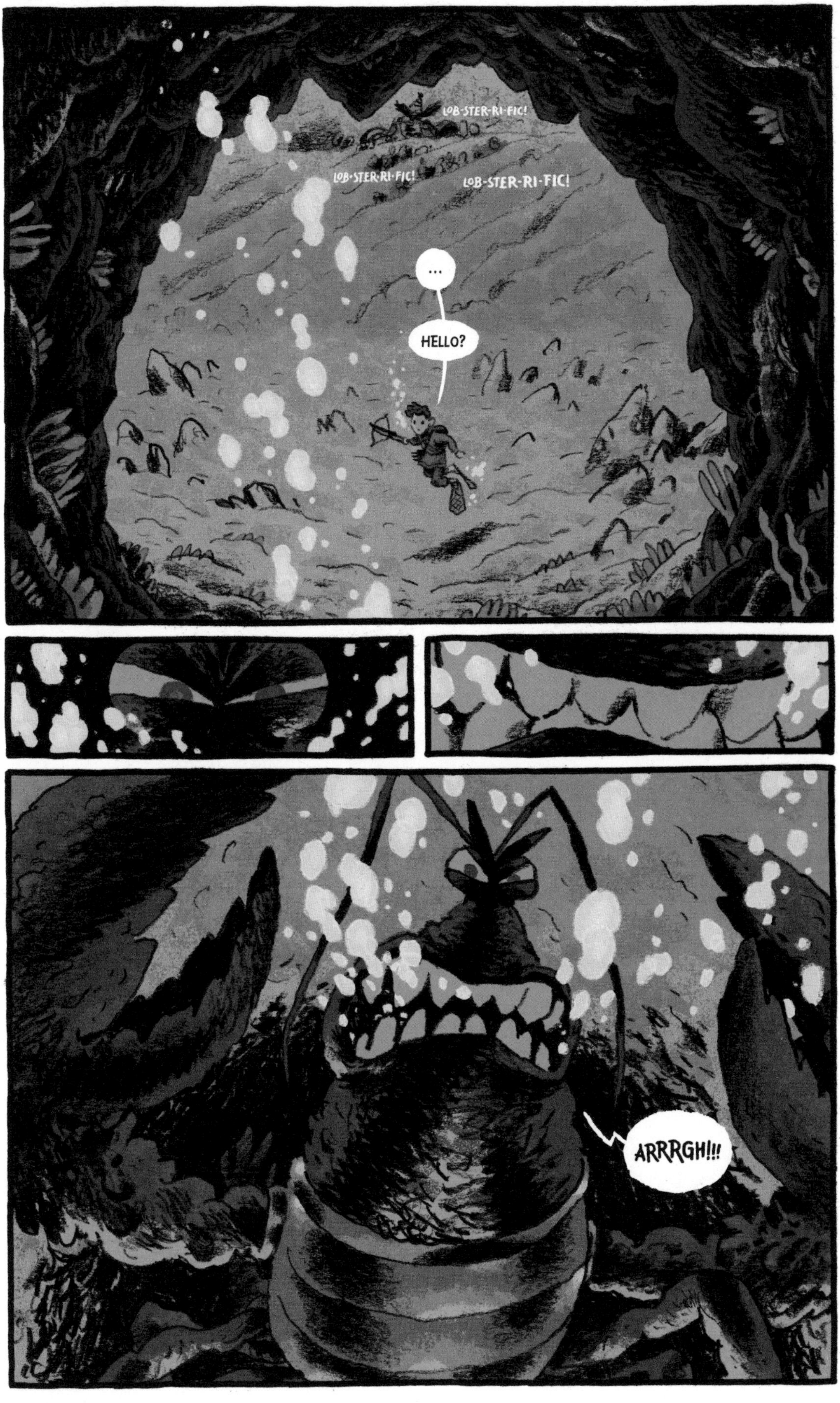
LOB-STER-RI-FIC!
LOB-STER-RI-FIC!
LOB-STER-RI-FIC!
...
HELLO?
ARRRGH!!!

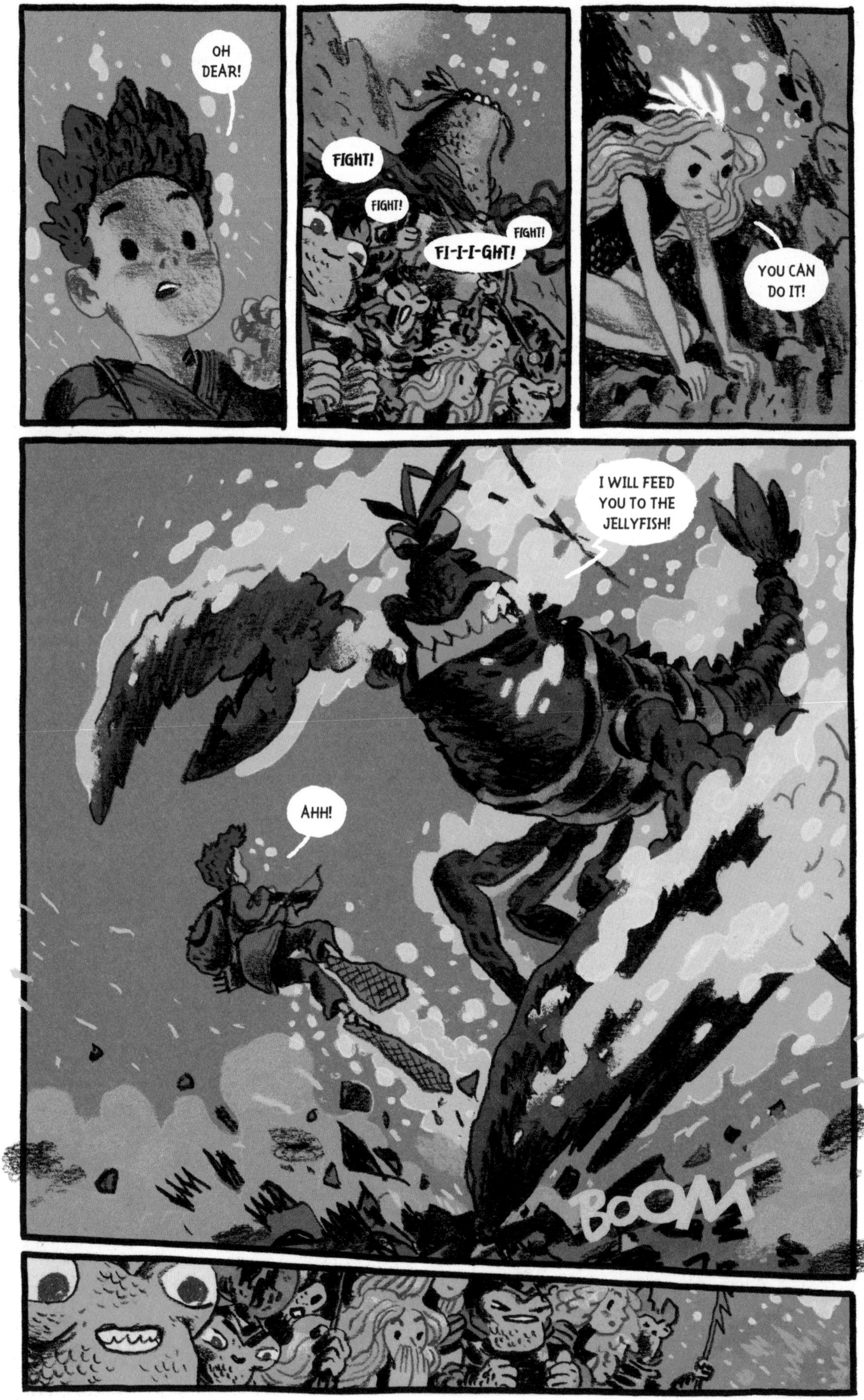
OH DEAR!
FIGHT!
FIGHT!
FI-I-I-GHT!
FIGHT!
YOU CAN DO IT!
I WILL FEED YOU TO THE JELLYFISH!
AHH!
BOOM!

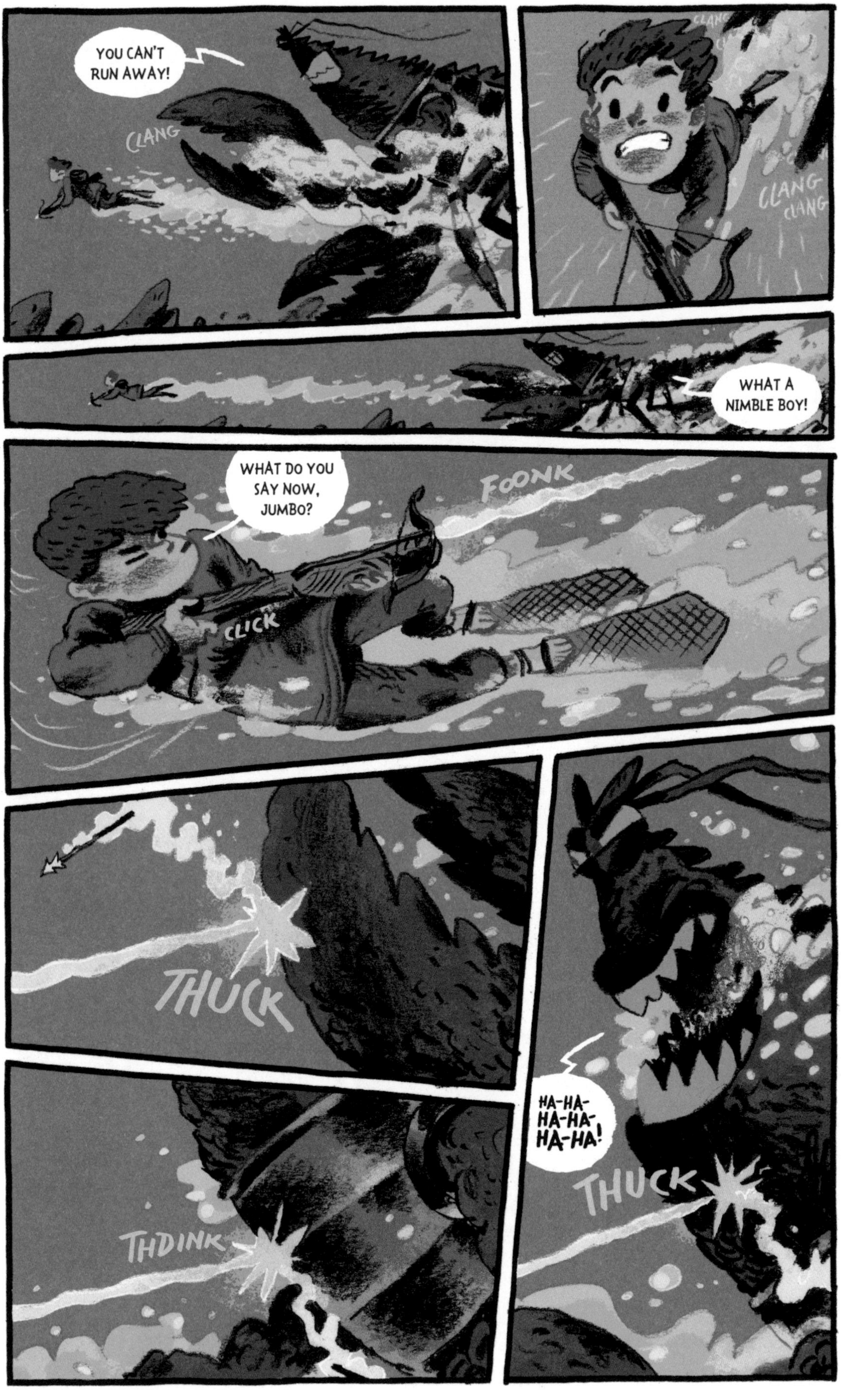
YOU CAN'T RUN AWAY!
CLANG
CLANG
CLANG
CLANG
WHAT A NIMBLE BOY!
WHAT DO YOU SAY NOW, JUMBO?
FOONK
CLICK
THUCK
HA-HA-HA-HA-HA-HA!
THUCK
THDINK

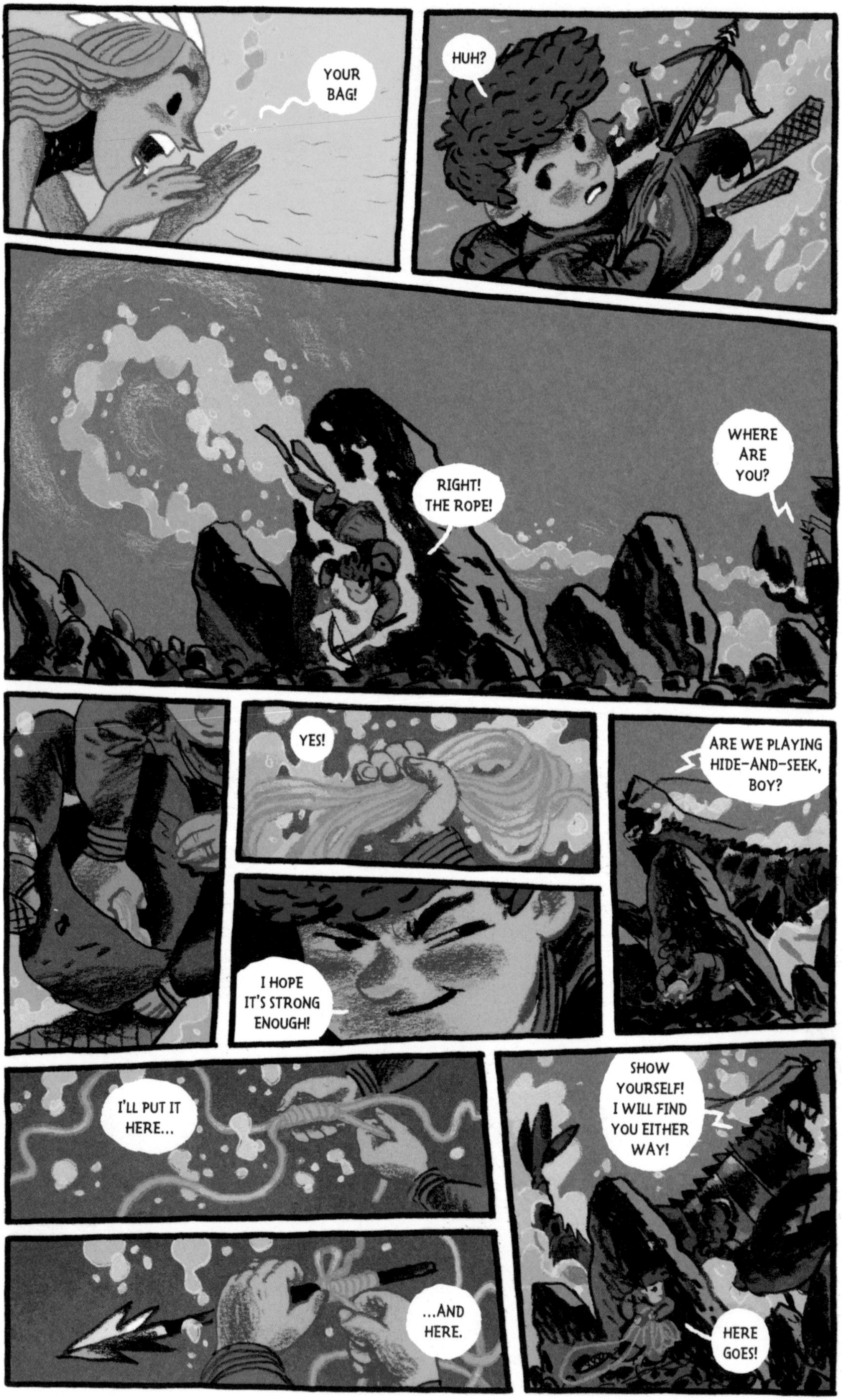
YOUR BAG!
HUH?
RIGHT! THE ROPE!
WHERE ARE YOU?
YES!
I HOPE IT'S STRONG ENOUGH!
ARE WE PLAYING HIDE-AND-SEEK, BOY?
I'LL PUT IT HERE...
...AND HERE.
SHOW YOURSELF! I WILL FIND YOU EITHER WAY!
HERE GOES!

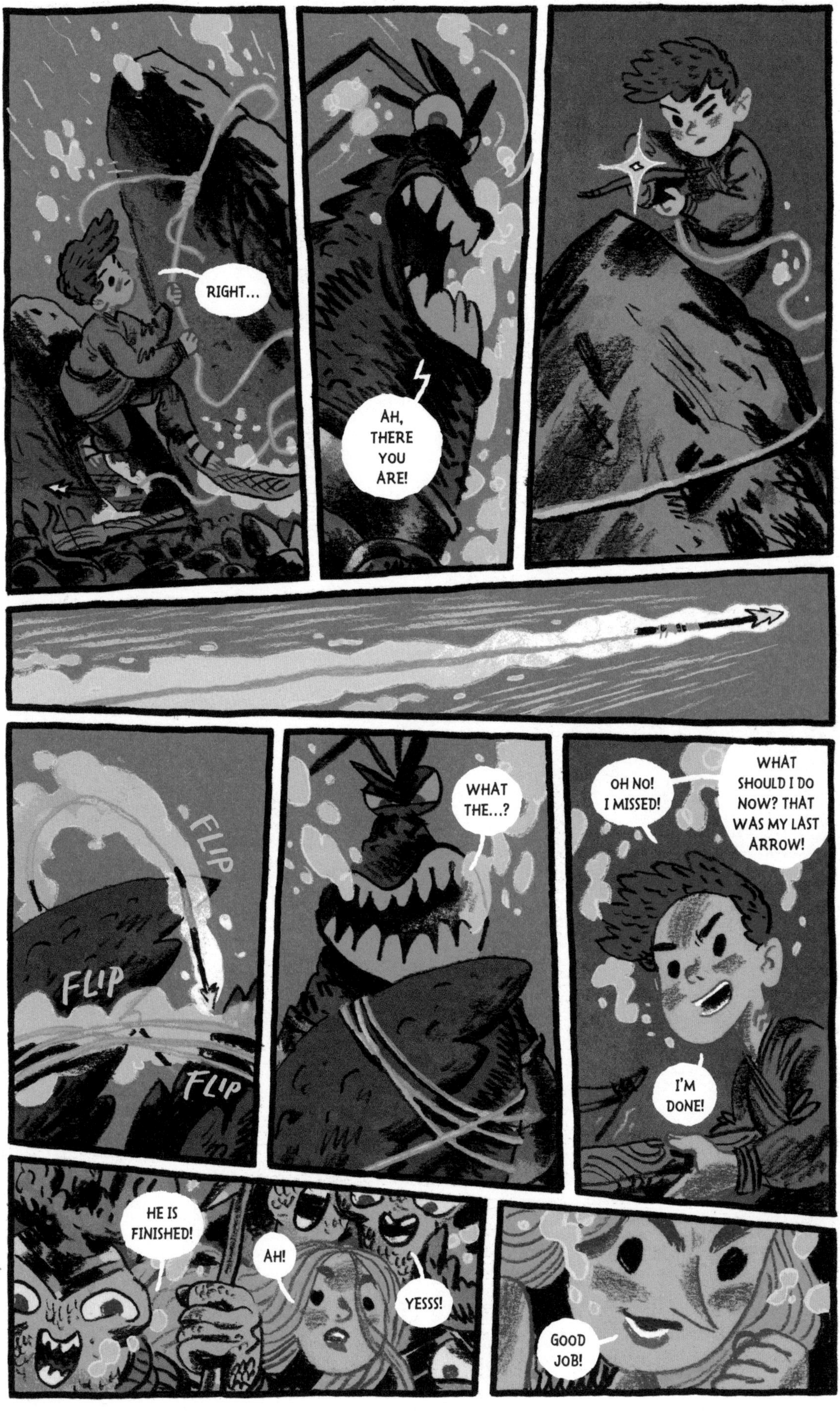
RIGHT...
AH, THERE YOU ARE!
FLIP
FLIP
FLIP
WHAT THE...?
OH NO! I MISSED!
WHAT SHOULD I DO NOW? THAT WAS MY LAST ARROW!
I'M DONE!
HE IS FINISHED!
AH!
YESSS!
GOOD JOB!

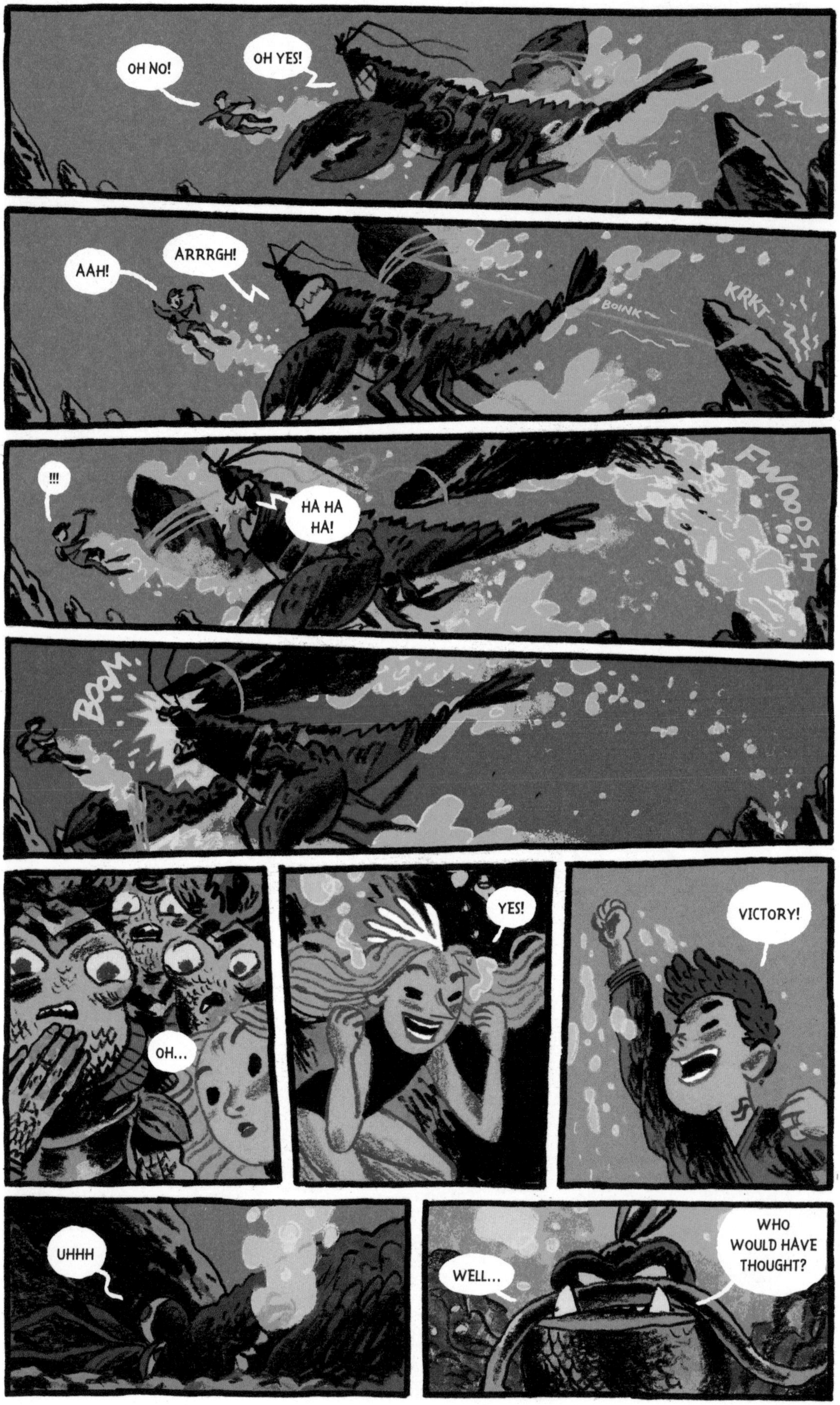
OH NO!
OH YES!
AAH!
ARRRGH!
BOINK
KRKT
!!!
HA HA HA!
FWOOOOSH
BOOM
OH...
YES!
VICTORY!
UHHH
WELL...
WHO WOULD HAVE THOUGHT?

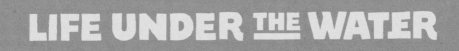

LIFE UNDER THE WATER

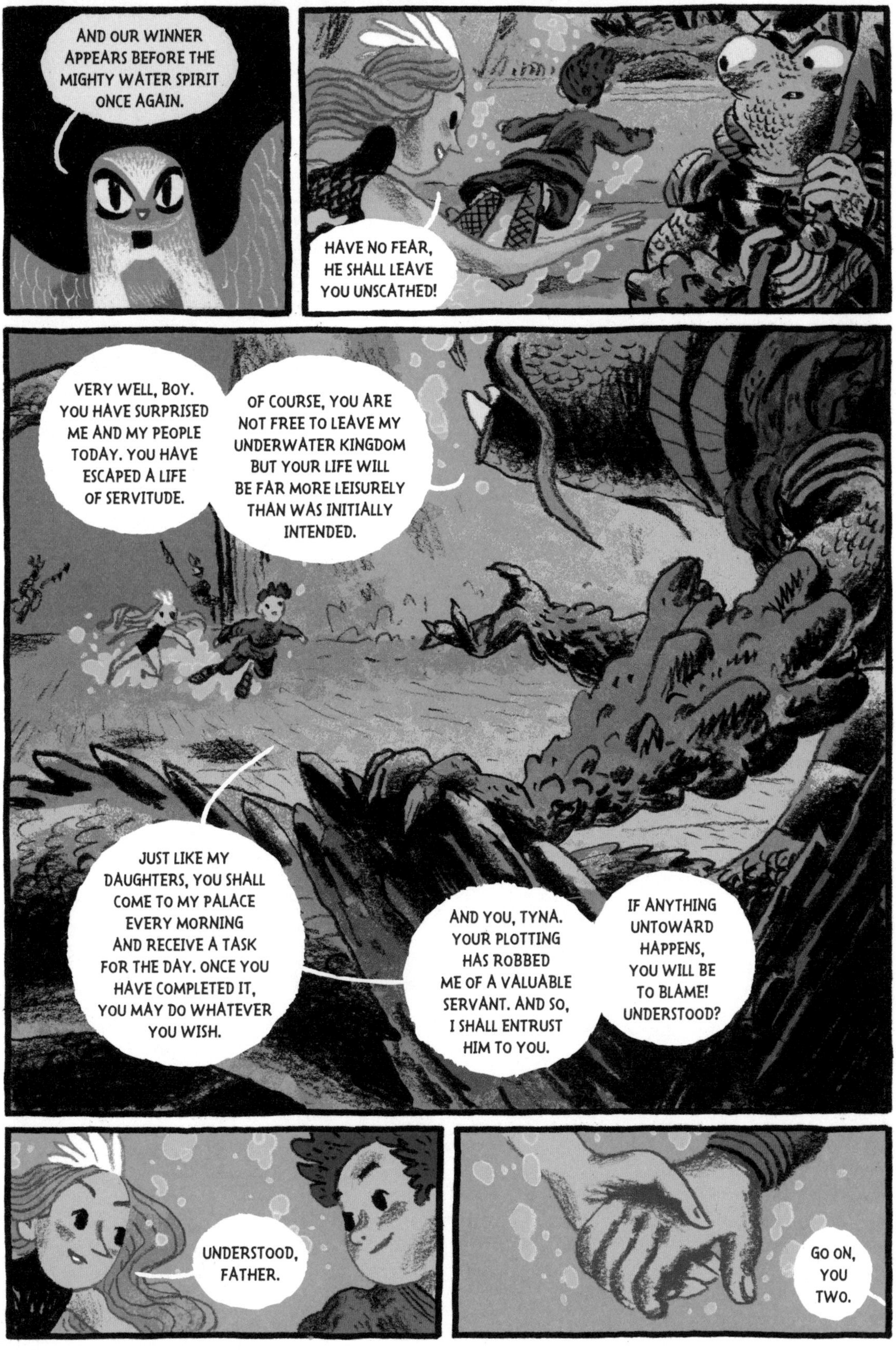
AND OUR WINNER APPEARS BEFORE THE MIGHTY WATER SPIRIT ONCE AGAIN.
HAVE NO FEAR, HE SHALL LEAVE YOU UNSCATHED!
VERY WELL, BOY. YOU HAVE SURPRISED ME AND MY PEOPLE TODAY. YOU HAVE ESCAPED A LIFE OF SERVITUDE.
OF COURSE, YOU ARE NOT FREE TO LEAVE MY UNDERWATER KINGDOM BUT YOUR LIFE WILL BE FAR MORE LEISURELY THAN WAS INITIALLY INTENDED.
JUST LIKE MY DAUGHTERS, YOU SHALL COME TO MY PALACE EVERY MORNING AND RECEIVE A TASK FOR THE DAY. ONCE YOU HAVE COMPLETED IT, YOU MAY DO WHATEVER YOU WISH.
AND YOU, TYNA. YOUR PLOTTING HAS ROBBED ME OF A VALUABLE SERVANT. AND SO, I SHALL ENTRUST HIM TO YOU.
IF ANYTHING UNTOWARD HAPPENS, YOU WILL BE TO BLAME! UNDERSTOOD?
UNDERSTOOD, FATHER.
GO ON, YOU TWO.

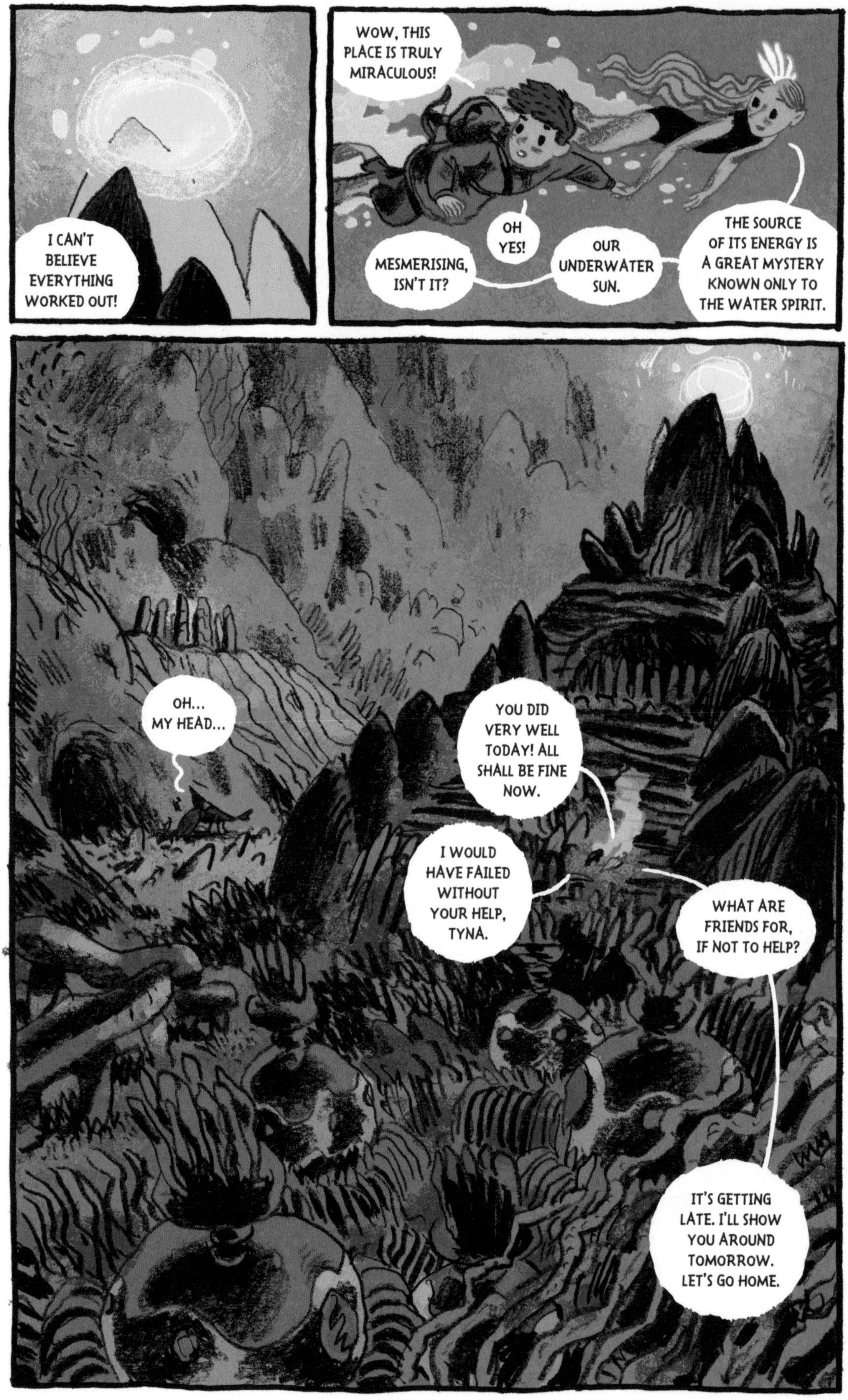
I CAN'T BELIEVE EVERYTHING WORKED OUT!
WOW, THIS PLACE IS TRULY MIRACULOUS!
MESMERISING, ISN'T IT?
OH YES!
OUR UNDERWATER SUN.
THE SOURCE OF ITS ENERGY IS A GREAT MYSTERY KNOWN ONLY TO THE WATER SPIRIT.
OH... MY HEAD...
YOU DID VERY WELL TODAY! ALL SHALL BE FINE NOW.
I WOULD HAVE FAILED WITHOUT YOUR HELP, TYNA.
WHAT ARE FRIENDS FOR, IF NOT TO HELP?
IT'S GETTING LATE. I'LL SHOW YOU AROUND TOMORROW. LET'S GO HOME.

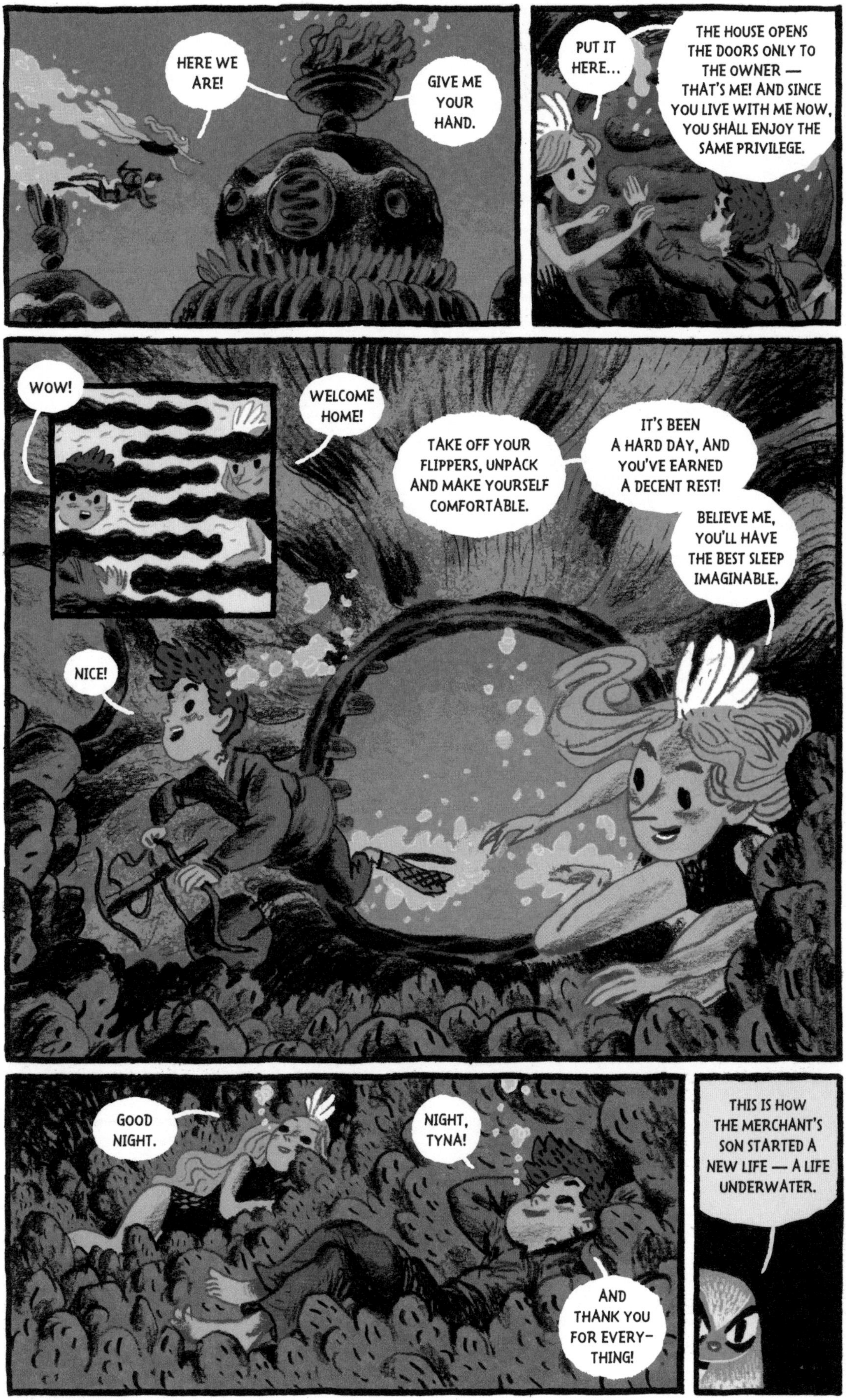
HERE WE ARE!
GIVE ME YOUR HAND.
PUT IT HERE...
THE HOUSE OPENS THE DOORS ONLY TO THE OWNER — THAT'S ME! AND SINCE YOU LIVE WITH ME NOW, YOU SHALL ENJOY THE SAME PRIVILEGE.
WOW!
WELCOME HOME!
NICE!
TAKE OFF YOUR FLIPPERS, UNPACK AND MAKE YOURSELF COMFORTABLE.
IT'S BEEN A HARD DAY, AND YOU'VE EARNED A DECENT REST!
BELIEVE ME, YOU'LL HAVE THE BEST SLEEP IMAGINABLE.
GOOD NIGHT.
NIGHT, TYNA!
AND THANK YOU FOR EVERY-THING!
THIS IS HOW THE MERCHANT'S SON STARTED A NEW LIFE — A LIFE UNDERWATER.

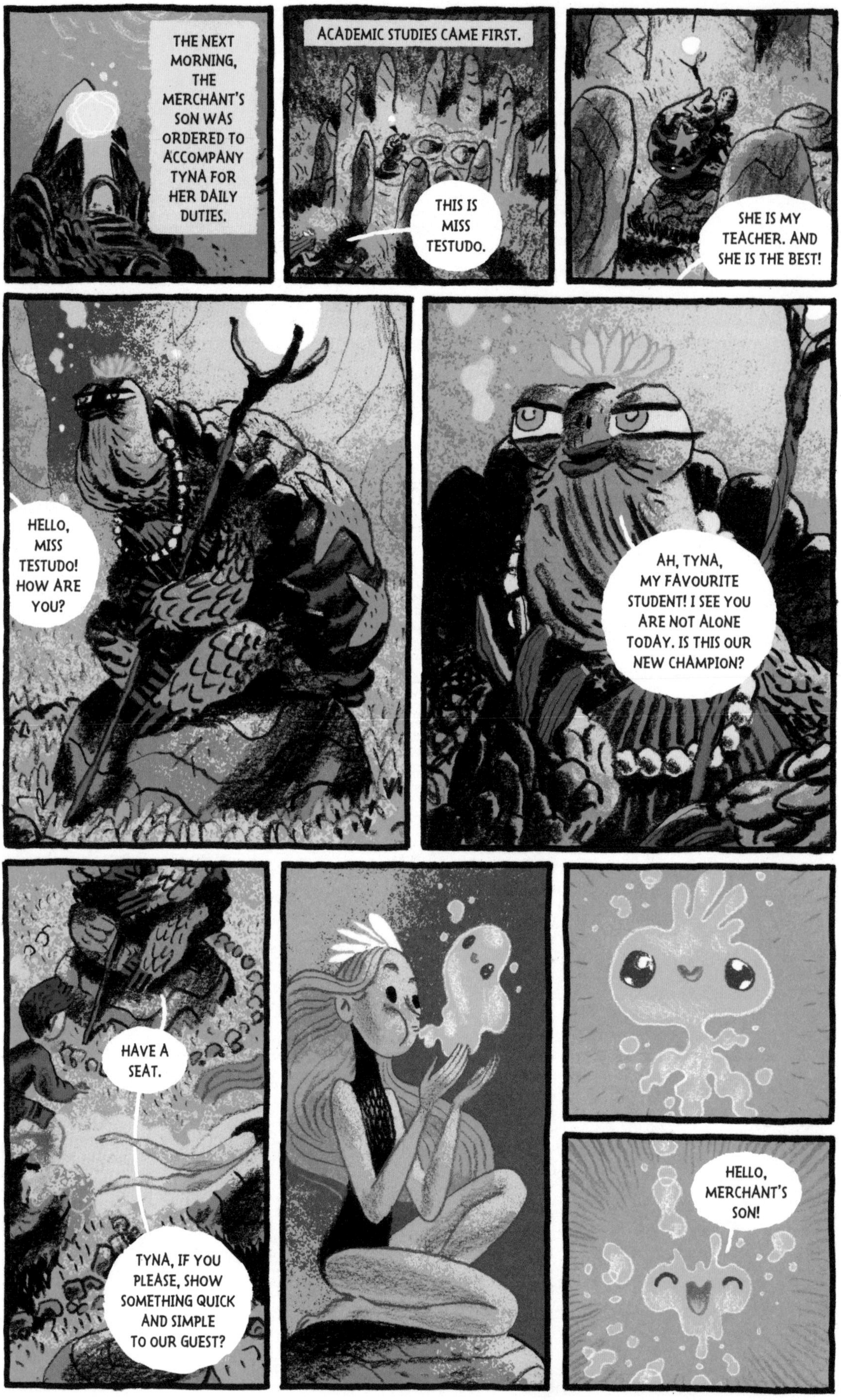
THE NEXT MORNING, THE MERCHANT'S SON WAS ORDERED TO ACCOMPANY TYNA FOR HER DAILY DUTIES.
ACADEMIC STUDIES CAME FIRST.
THIS IS MISS TESTUDO.
SHE IS MY TEACHER. AND SHE IS THE BEST!
HELLO, MISS TESTUDO! HOW ARE YOU?
AH, TYNA, MY FAVOURITE STUDENT! I SEE YOU ARE NOT ALONE TODAY. IS THIS OUR NEW CHAMPION?
HAVE A SEAT.
TYNA, IF YOU PLEASE, SHOW SOMETHING QUICK AND SIMPLE TO OUR GUEST?
HELLO, MERCHANT'S SON!

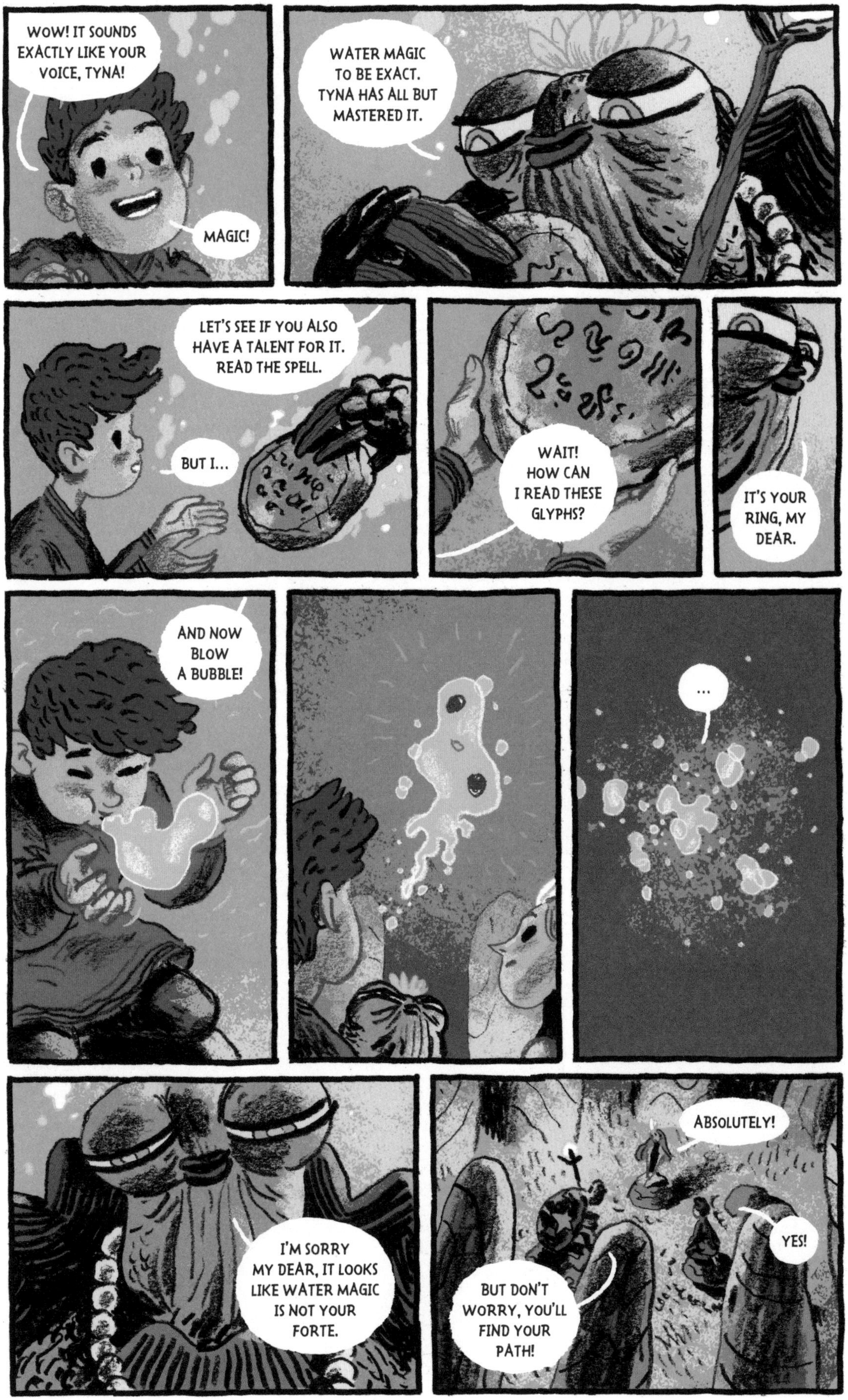
WOW! IT SOUNDS EXACTLY LIKE YOUR VOICE, TYNA!
MAGIC!
WATER MAGIC TO BE EXACT. TYNA HAS ALL BUT MASTERED IT.
LET'S SEE IF YOU ALSO HAVE A TALENT FOR IT. READ THE SPELL.
BUT I...
WAIT! HOW CAN I READ THESE GLYPHS?
IT'S YOUR RING, MY DEAR.
AND NOW BLOW A BUBBLE!
...
I'M SORRY MY DEAR, IT LOOKS LIKE WATER MAGIC IS NOT YOUR FORTE.
ABSOLUTELY!
YES!
BUT DON'T WORRY, YOU'LL FIND YOUR PATH!

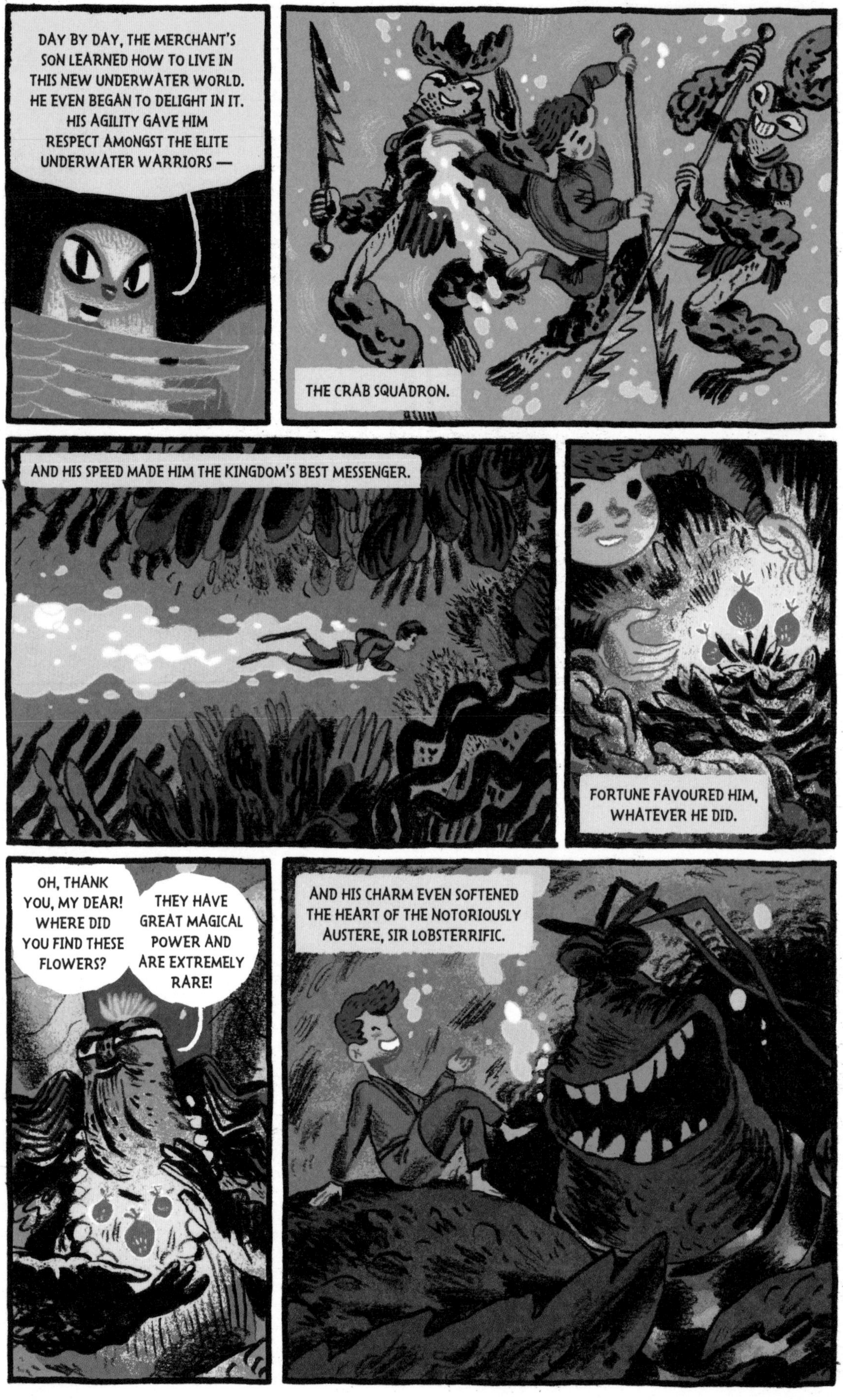
DAY BY DAY, THE MERCHANT'S SON LEARNED HOW TO LIVE IN THIS NEW UNDERWATER WORLD. HE EVEN BEGAN TO DELIGHT IN IT. HIS AGILITY GAVE HIM RESPECT AMONGST THE ELITE UNDERWATER WARRIORS —
THE CRAB SQUADRON.
AND HIS SPEED MADE HIM THE KINGDOM'S BEST MESSENGER.
FORTUNE FAVOURED HIM, WHATEVER HE DID.
OH, THANK YOU, MY DEAR! WHERE DID YOU FIND THESE FLOWERS?
THEY HAVE GREAT MAGICAL POWER AND ARE EXTREMELY RARE!
AND HIS CHARM EVEN SOFTENED THE HEART OF THE NOTORIOUSLY AUSTERE, SIR LOBSTERRIFIC.

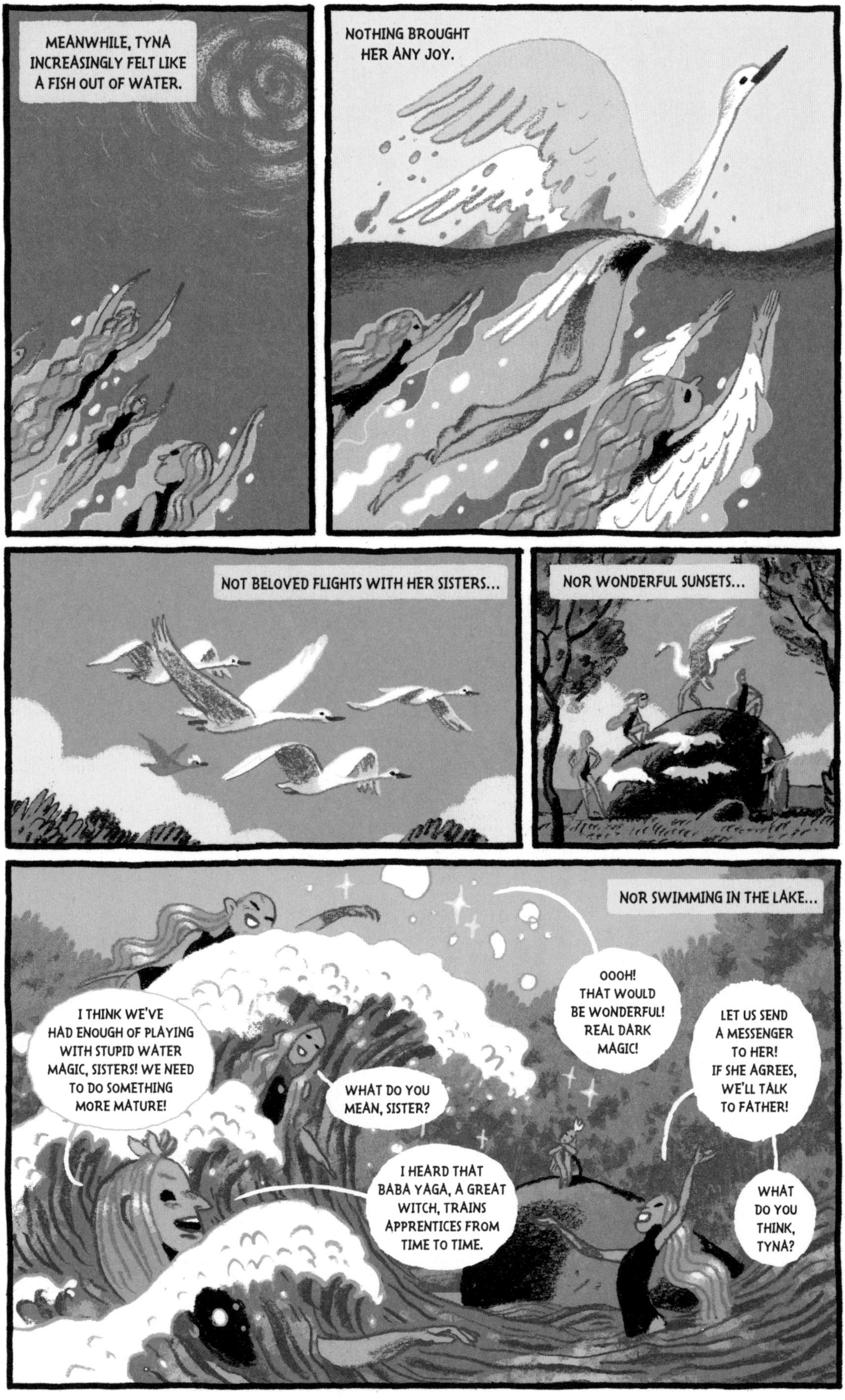
MEANWHILE, TYNA INCREASINGLY FELT LIKE A FISH OUT OF WATER.
NOTHING BROUGHT HER ANY JOY.
NOT BELOVED FLIGHTS WITH HER SISTERS...
NOR WONDERFUL SUNSETS...
NOR SWIMMING IN THE LAKE...
I THINK WE'VE HAD ENOUGH OF PLAYING WITH STUPID WATER MAGIC, SISTERS! WE NEED TO DO SOMETHING MORE MATURE!
WHAT DO YOU MEAN, SISTER?
I HEARD THAT BABA YAGA, A GREAT WITCH, TRAINS APPRENTICES FROM TIME TO TIME.
OOOH! THAT WOULD BE WONDERFUL! REAL DARK MAGIC!
LET US SEND A MESSENGER TO HER! IF SHE AGREES, WE'LL TALK TO FATHER!
WHAT DO YOU THINK, TYNA?

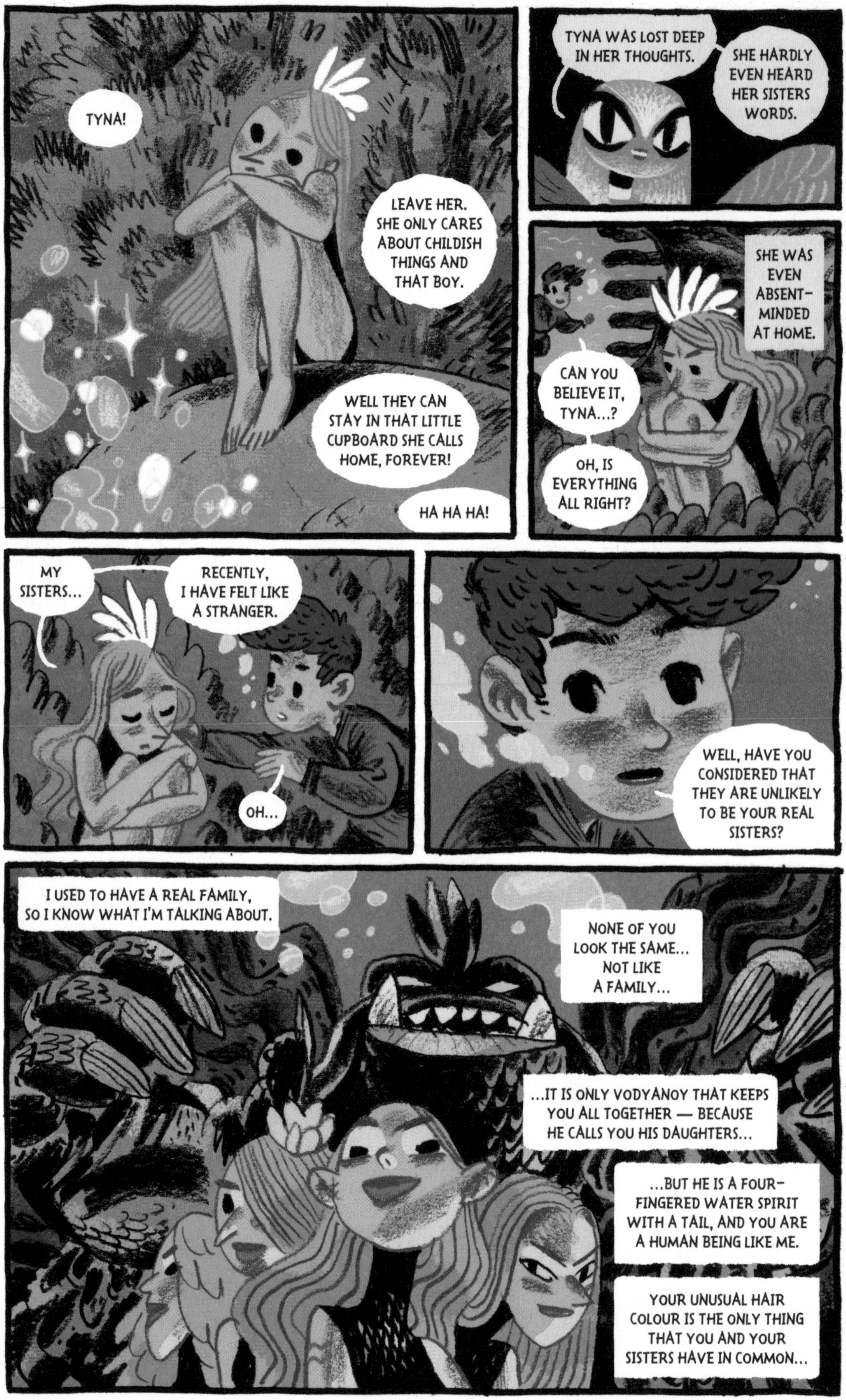
TYNA!
LEAVE HER. SHE ONLY CARES ABOUT CHILDISH THINGS AND THAT BOY.
WELL THEY CAN STAY IN THAT LITTLE CUPBOARD SHE CALLS HOME, FOREVER!
HA HA HA!
TYNA WAS LOST DEEP IN HER THOUGHTS.
SHE HARDLY EVEN HEARD HER SISTERS WORDS.
SHE WAS EVEN ABSENT-MINDED AT HOME.
CAN YOU BELIEVE IT, TYNA...?
OH, IS EVERYTHING ALL RIGHT?
MY SISTERS...
RECENTLY, I HAVE FELT LIKE A STRANGER.
OH...
WELL, HAVE YOU CONSIDERED THAT THEY ARE UNLIKELY TO BE YOUR REAL SISTERS?
I USED TO HAVE A REAL FAMILY, SO I KNOW WHAT I'M TALKING ABOUT.
NONE OF YOU LOOK THE SAME... NOT LIKE A FAMILY...
...IT IS ONLY VODYANOY THAT KEEPS YOU ALL TOGETHER — BECAUSE HE CALLS YOU HIS DAUGHTERS...
...BUT HE IS A FOUR-FINGERED WATER SPIRIT WITH A TAIL, AND YOU ARE A HUMAN BEING LIKE ME.
YOUR UNUSUAL HAIR COLOUR IS THE ONLY THING THAT YOU AND YOUR SISTERS HAVE IN COMMON...

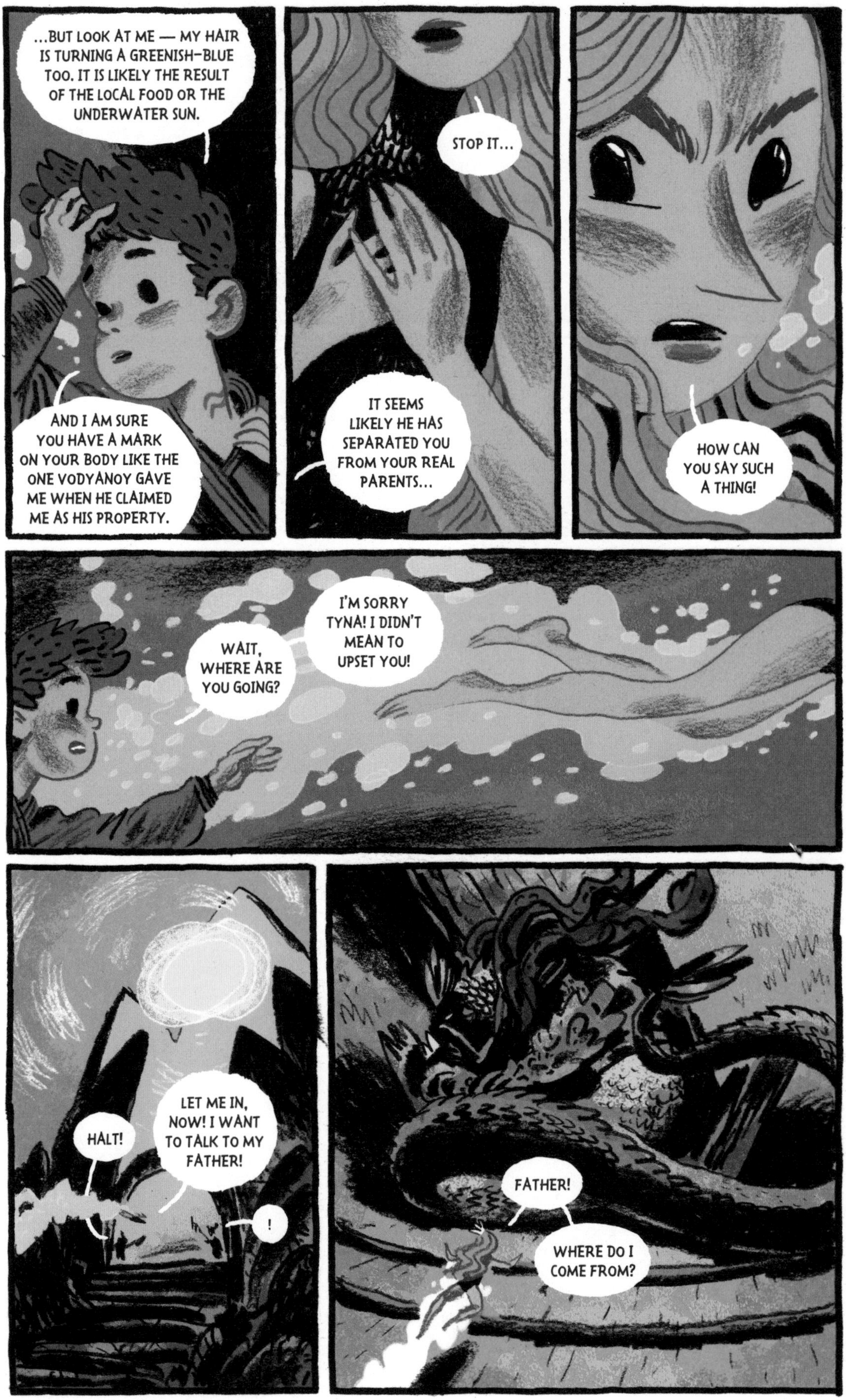
...BUT LOOK AT ME — MY HAIR IS TURNING A GREENISH-BLUE TOO. IT IS LIKELY THE RESULT OF THE LOCAL FOOD OR THE UNDERWATER SUN.
AND I AM SURE YOU HAVE A MARK ON YOUR BODY LIKE THE ONE VODYANOY GAVE ME WHEN HE CLAIMED ME AS HIS PROPERTY.
STOP IT...
IT SEEMS LIKELY HE HAS SEPARATED YOU FROM YOUR REAL PARENTS...
HOW CAN YOU SAY SUCH A THING!
WAIT, WHERE ARE YOU GOING?
I'M SORRY TYNA! I DIDN'T MEAN TO UPSET YOU!
HALT!
LET ME IN, NOW! I WANT TO TALK TO MY FATHER!
!
FATHER!
WHERE DO I COME FROM?

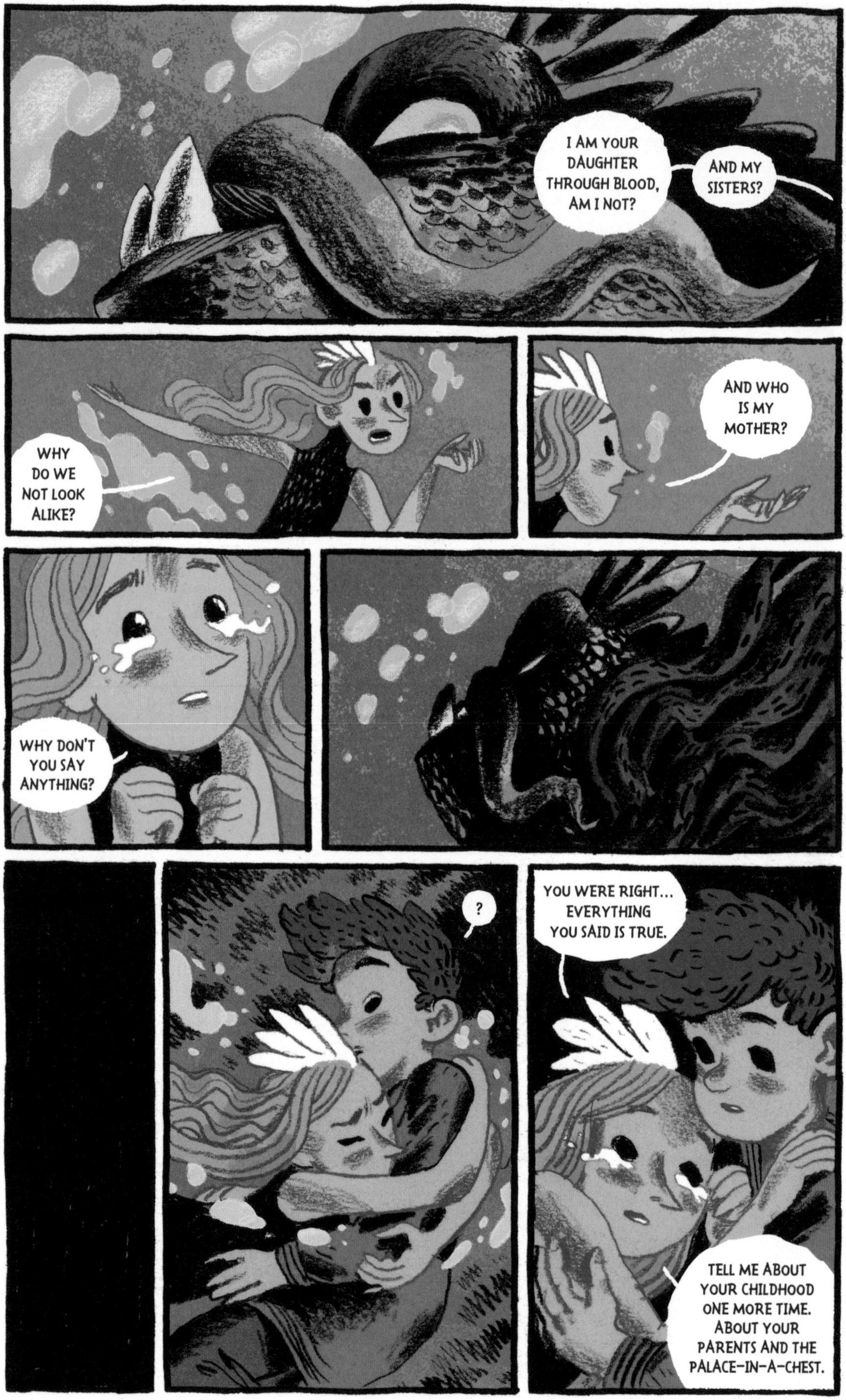
I AM YOUR DAUGHTER THROUGH BLOOD, AM I NOT?
AND MY SISTERS?
WHY DO WE NOT LOOK ALIKE?
AND WHO IS MY MOTHER?
WHY DON'T YOU SAY ANYTHING?
?
YOU WERE RIGHT... EVERYTHING YOU SAID IS TRUE.
TELL ME ABOUT YOUR CHILDHOOD ONE MORE TIME. ABOUT YOUR PARENTS AND THE PALACE-IN-A-CHEST.

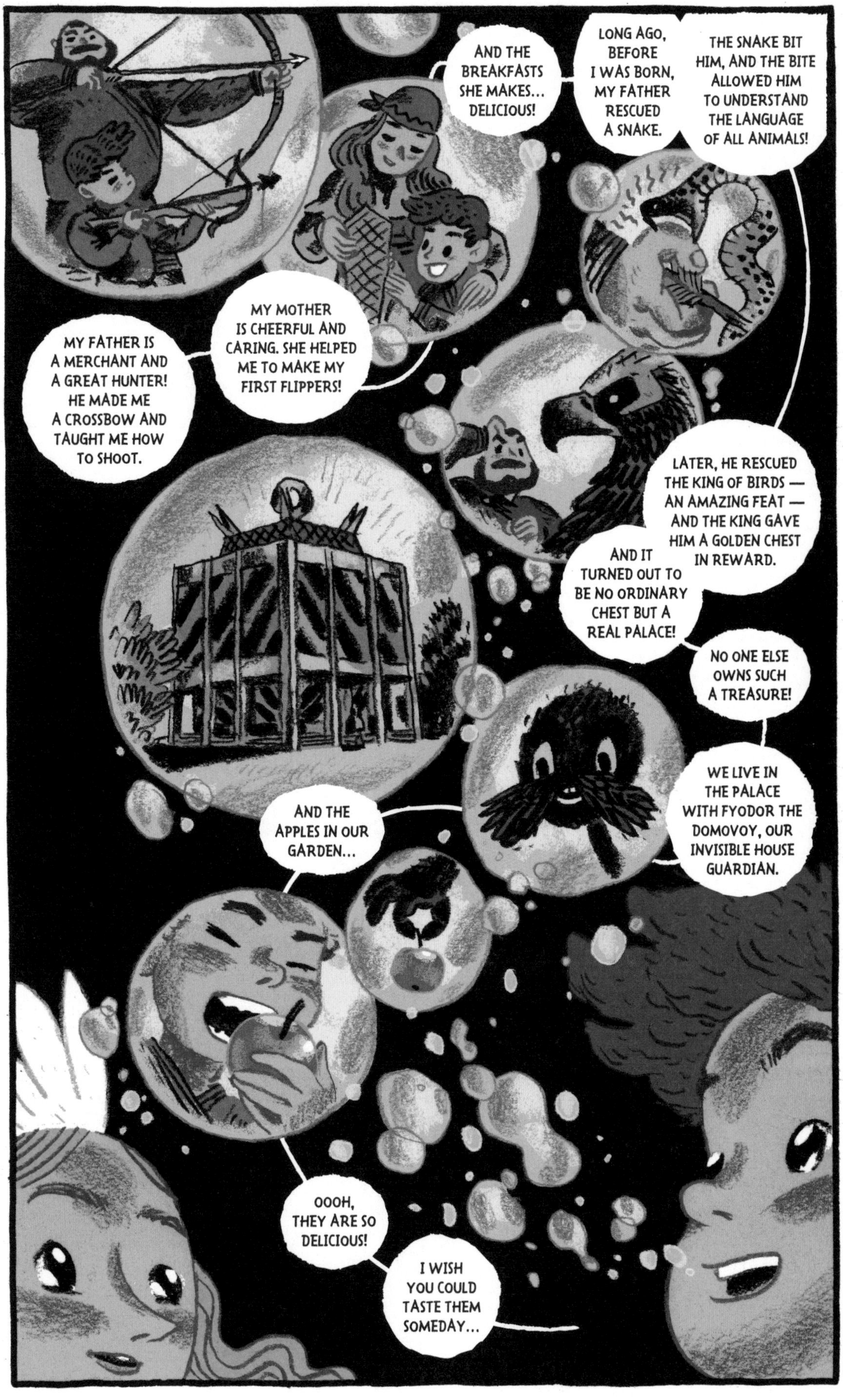
MY FATHER IS A MERCHANT AND A GREAT HUNTER! HE MADE ME A CROSSBOW AND TAUGHT ME HOW TO SHOOT.
MY MOTHER IS CHEERFUL AND CARING. SHE HELPED ME TO MAKE MY FIRST FLIPPERS!
AND THE BREAKFASTS SHE MAKES... DELICIOUS!
LONG AGO, BEFORE I WAS BORN, MY FATHER RESCUED A SNAKE.
THE SNAKE BIT HIM, AND THE BITE ALLOWED HIM TO UNDERSTAND THE LANGUAGE OF ALL ANIMALS!
LATER, HE RESCUED THE KING OF BIRDS — AN AMAZING FEAT — AND THE KING GAVE HIM A GOLDEN CHEST IN REWARD.
AND IT TURNED OUT TO BE NO ORDINARY CHEST BUT A REAL PALACE!
NO ONE ELSE OWNS SUCH A TREASURE!
WE LIVE IN THE PALACE WITH FYODOR THE DOMOVOY, OUR INVISIBLE HOUSE GUARDIAN.
AND THE APPLES IN OUR GARDEN...
OOOH, THEY ARE SO DELICIOUS!
I WISH YOU COULD TASTE THEM SOMEDAY...

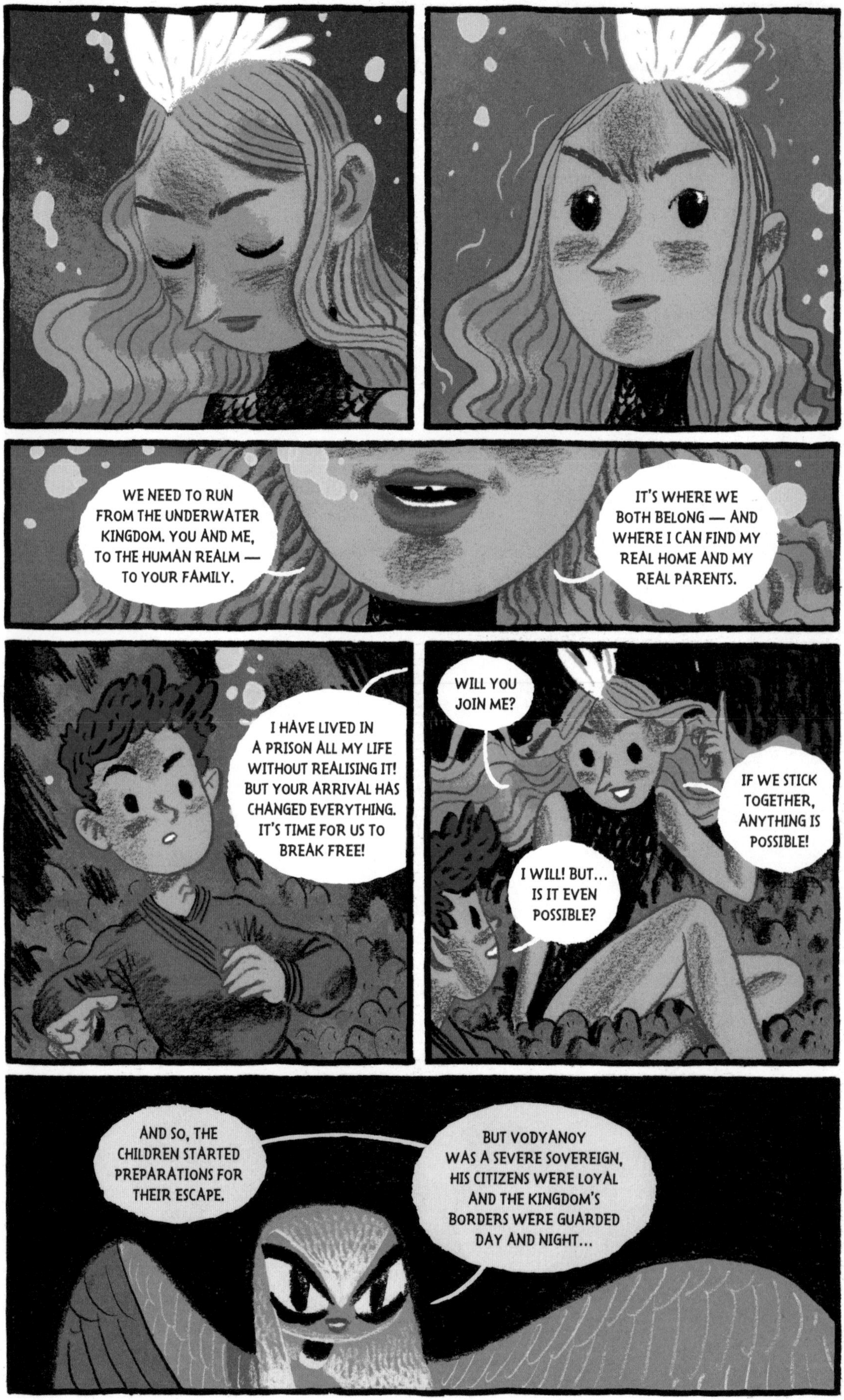
WE NEED TO RUN FROM THE UNDERWATER KINGDOM. YOU AND ME, TO THE HUMAN REALM — TO YOUR FAMILY.
IT'S WHERE WE BOTH BELONG — AND WHERE I CAN FIND MY REAL HOME AND MY REAL PARENTS.
I HAVE LIVED IN A PRISON ALL MY LIFE WITHOUT REALISING IT! BUT YOUR ARRIVAL HAS CHANGED EVERYTHING. IT'S TIME FOR US TO BREAK FREE!
WILL YOU JOIN ME?
IF WE STICK TOGETHER, ANYTHING IS POSSIBLE!
I WILL! BUT... IS IT EVEN POSSIBLE?
AND SO, THE CHILDREN STARTED PREPARATIONS FOR THEIR ESCAPE.
BUT VODYANOY WAS A SEVERE SOVEREIGN, HIS CITIZENS WERE LOYAL AND THE KINGDOM'S BORDERS WERE GUARDED DAY AND NIGHT...

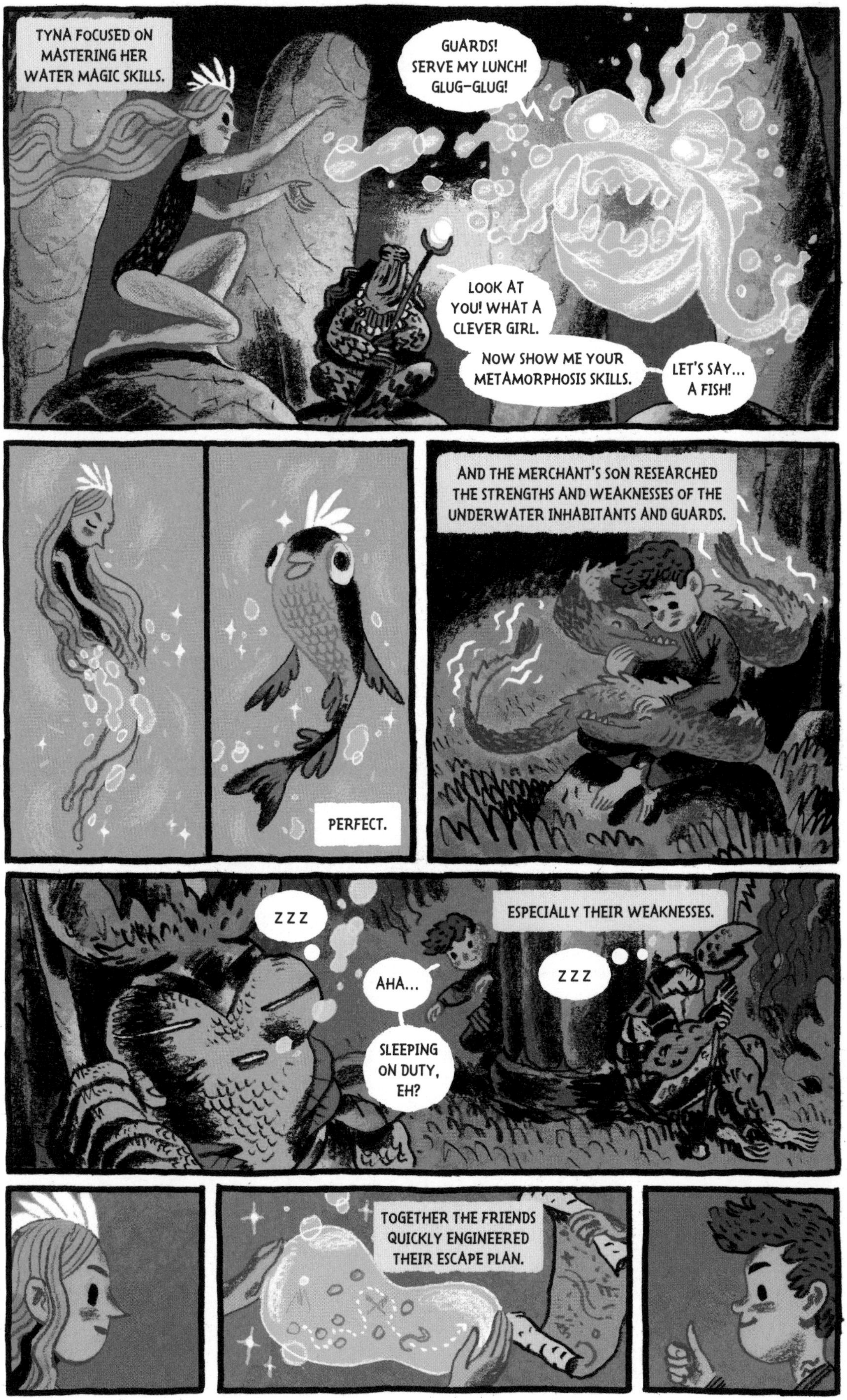
TYNA FOCUSED ON MASTERING HER WATER MAGIC SKILLS.
GUARDS! SERVE MY LUNCH! GLUG-GLUG!
LOOK AT YOU! WHAT A CLEVER GIRL.
NOW SHOW ME YOUR METAMORPHOSIS SKILLS.
LET'S SAY... A FISH!
PERFECT.
AND THE MERCHANT'S SON RESEARCHED THE STRENGTHS AND WEAKNESSES OF THE UNDERWATER INHABITANTS AND GUARDS.
ZZZ
ESPECIALLY THEIR WEAKNESSES.
AHA...
ZZZ
SLEEPING ON DUTY, EH?
TOGETHER THE FRIENDS QUICKLY ENGINEERED THEIR ESCAPE PLAN.

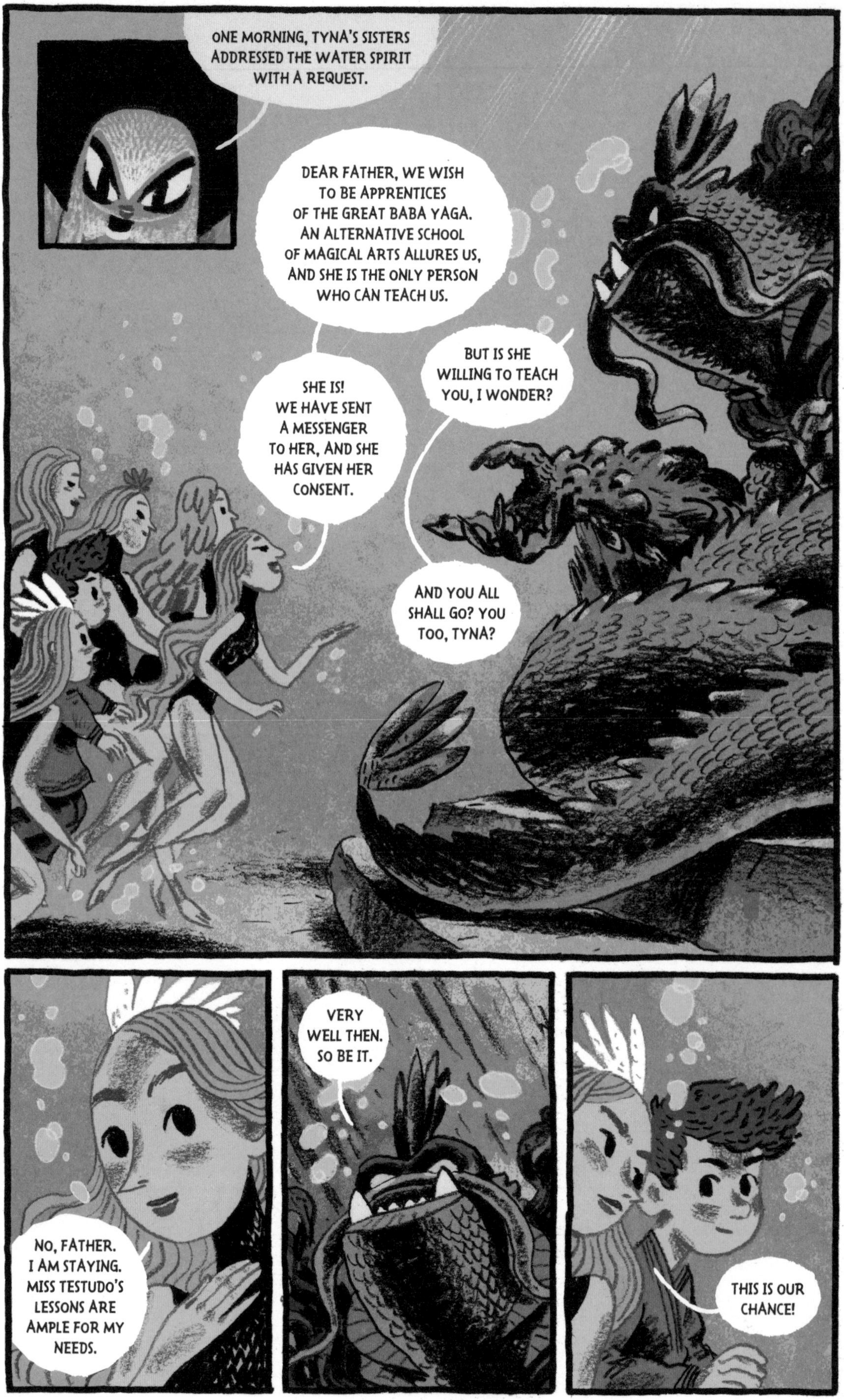
ONE MORNING, TYNA'S SISTERS ADDRESSED THE WATER SPIRIT WITH A REQUEST.
DEAR FATHER, WE WISH TO BE APPRENTICES OF THE GREAT BABA YAGA. AN ALTERNATIVE SCHOOL OF MAGICAL ARTS ALLURES US, AND SHE IS THE ONLY PERSON WHO CAN TEACH US.
BUT IS SHE WILLING TO TEACH YOU, I WONDER?
SHE IS! WE HAVE SENT A MESSENGER TO HER, AND SHE HAS GIVEN HER CONSENT.
AND YOU ALL SHALL GO? YOU TOO, TYNA?
NO, FATHER. I AM STAYING. MISS TESTUDO'S LESSONS ARE AMPLE FOR MY NEEDS.
VERY WELL THEN. SO BE IT.
THIS IS OUR CHANCE!

THE CHASE

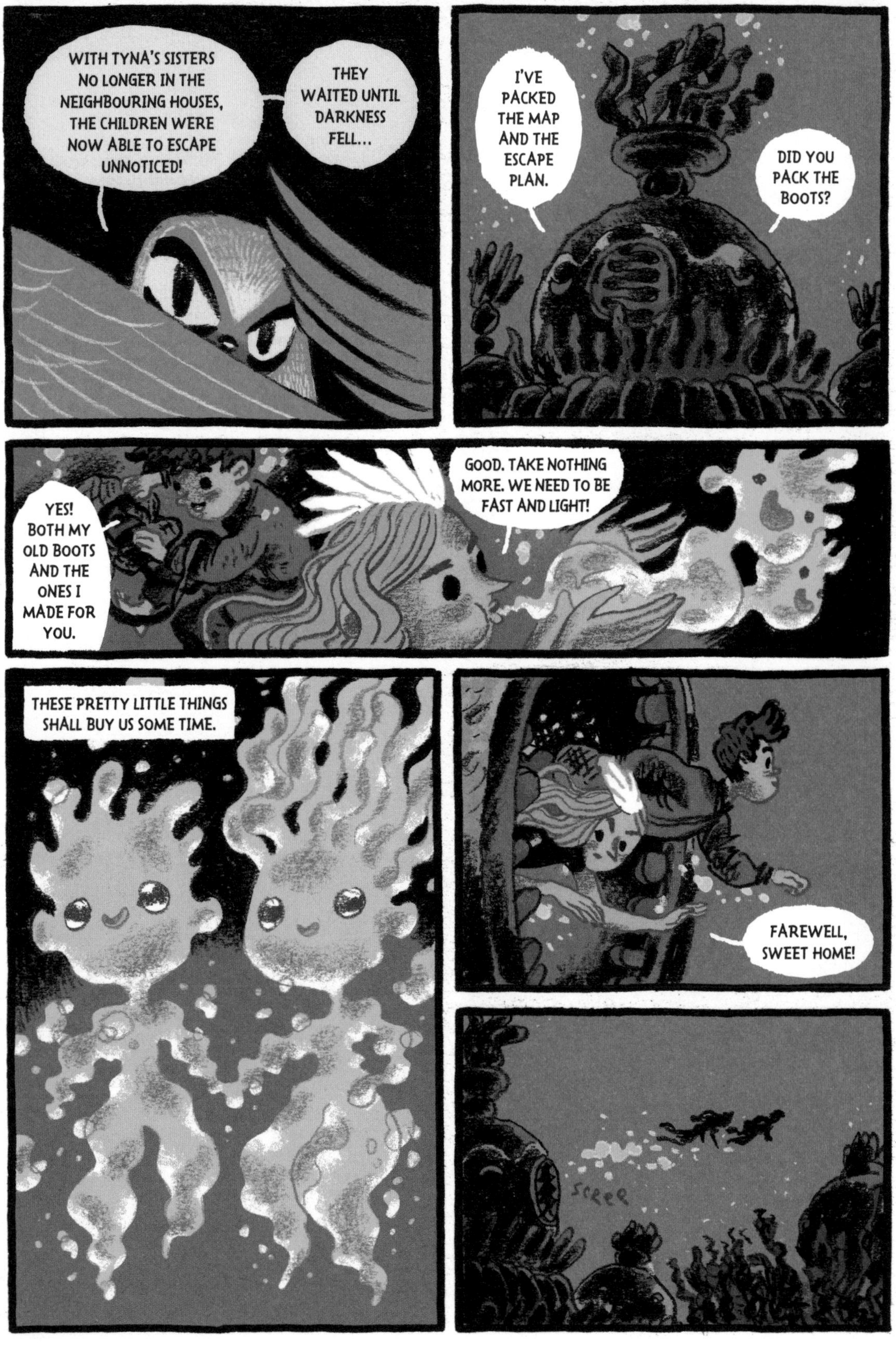
WITH TYNA'S SISTERS NO LONGER IN THE NEIGHBOURING HOUSES, THE CHILDREN WERE NOW ABLE TO ESCAPE UNNOTICED!
THEY WAITED UNTIL DARKNESS FELL...
I'VE PACKED THE MAP AND THE ESCAPE PLAN.
DID YOU PACK THE BOOTS?
YES! BOTH MY OLD BOOTS AND THE ONES I MADE FOR YOU.
GOOD. TAKE NOTHING MORE. WE NEED TO BE FAST AND LIGHT!
THESE PRETTY LITTLE THINGS SHALL BUY US SOME TIME.
FAREWELL, SWEET HOME!
SCREE

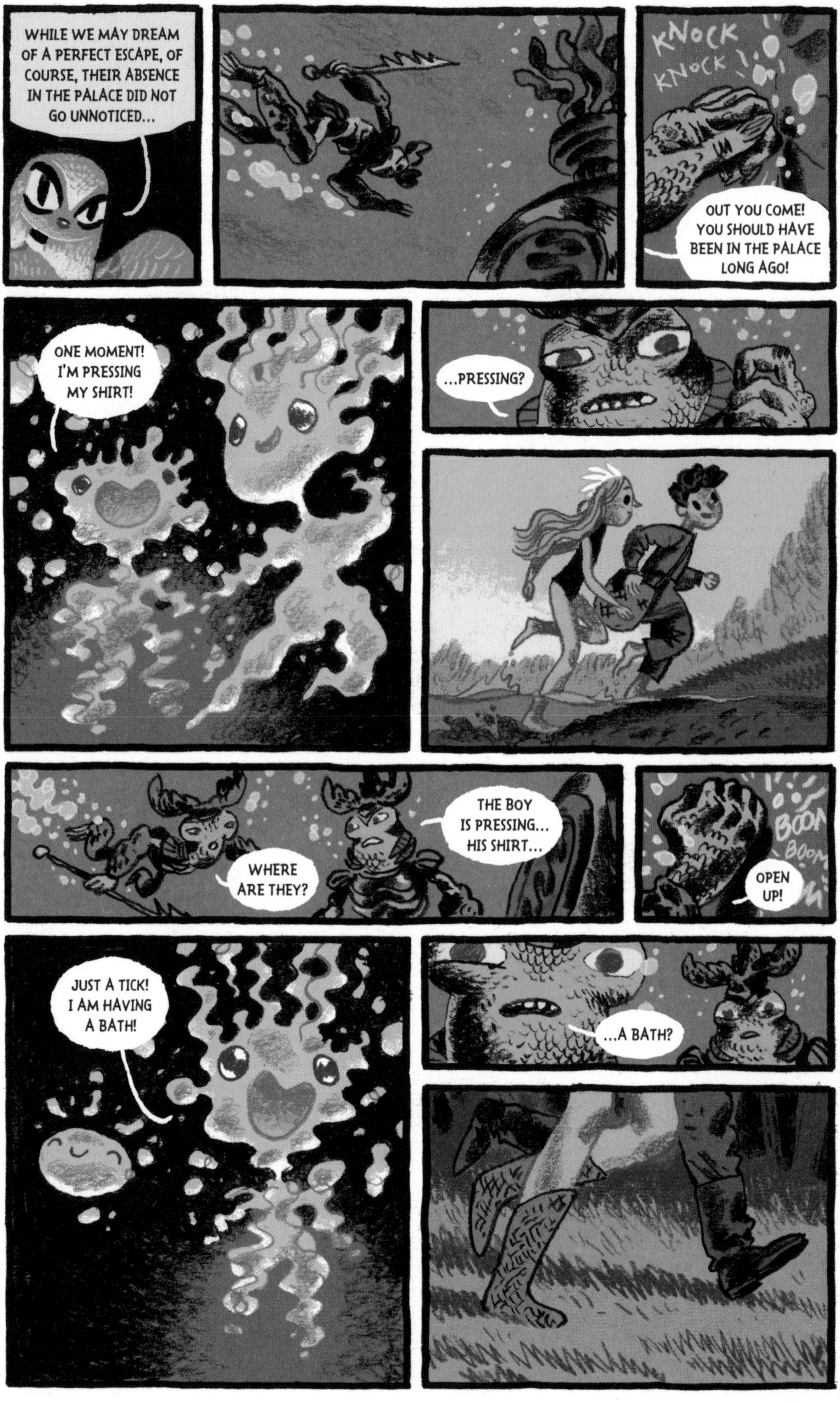
WHILE WE MAY DREAM OF A PERFECT ESCAPE, OF COURSE, THEIR ABSENCE IN THE PALACE DID NOT GO UNNOTICED...
KNOCK KNOCK
OUT YOU COME! YOU SHOULD HAVE BEEN IN THE PALACE LONG AGO!
ONE MOMENT! I'M PRESSING MY SHIRT!
...PRESSING?
WHERE ARE THEY?
THE BOY IS PRESSING... HIS SHIRT...
BOOM BOOM
OPEN UP!
JUST A TICK! I AM HAVING A BATH!
...A BATH?

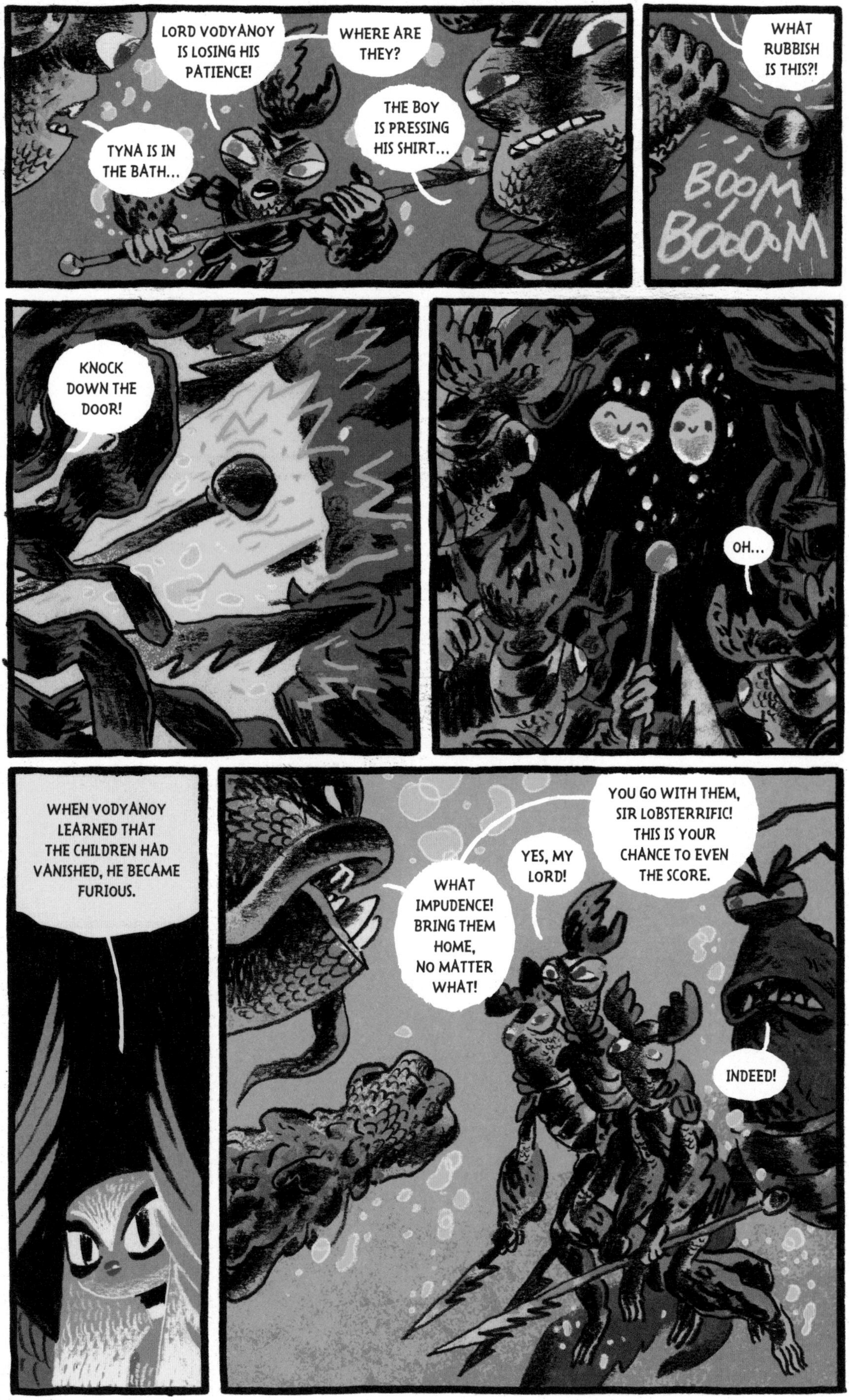
LORD VODYANOY IS LOSING HIS PATIENCE!
WHERE ARE THEY?
TYNA IS IN THE BATH...
THE BOY IS PRESSING HIS SHIRT...
WHAT RUBBISH IS THIS?!
BOOM BOOOOM
KNOCK DOWN THE DOOR!
OH...
WHEN VODYANOY LEARNED THAT THE CHILDREN HAD VANISHED, HE BECAME FURIOUS.
YOU GO WITH THEM, SIR LOBSTERRIFIC! THIS IS YOUR CHANCE TO EVEN THE SCORE.
YES, MY LORD!
WHAT IMPUDENCE! BRING THEM HOME, NO MATTER WHAT!
INDEED!

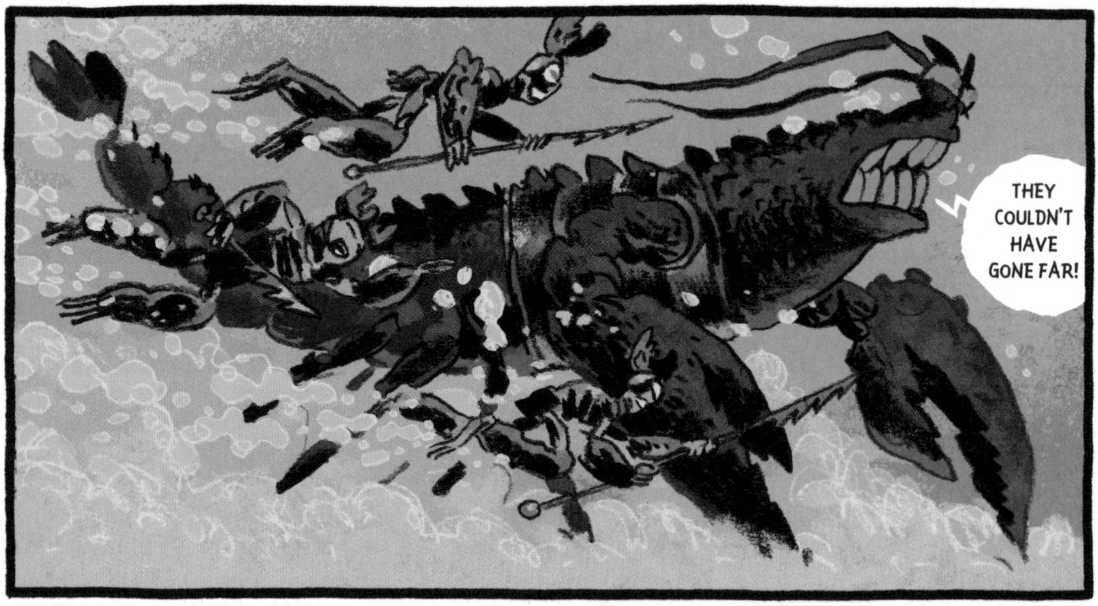
THEY COULDN'T HAVE GONE FAR!

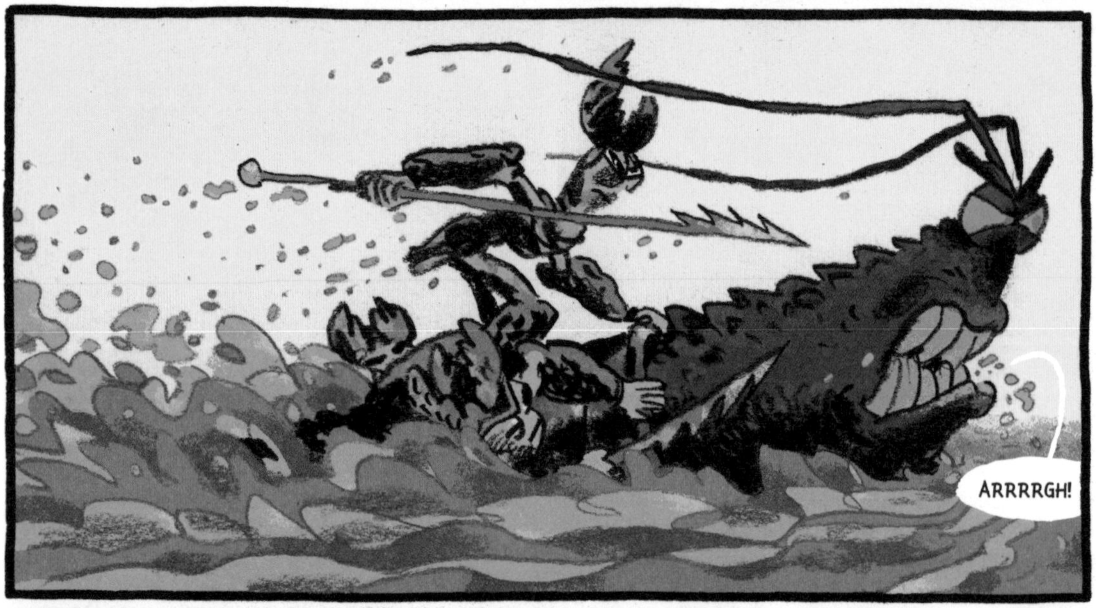
ARRRRGH!

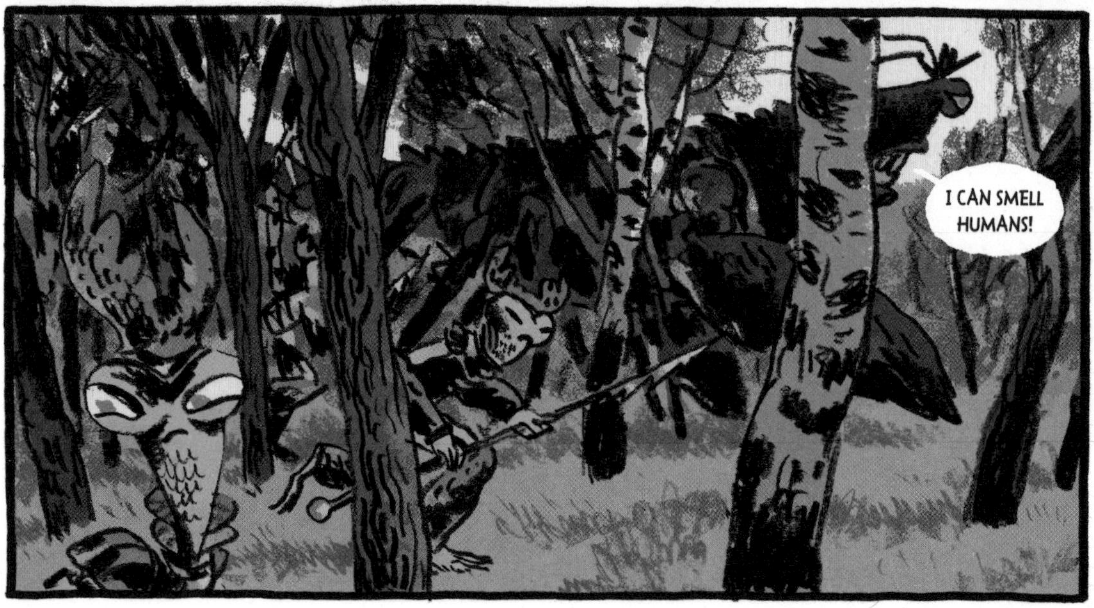
I CAN SMELL HUMANS!

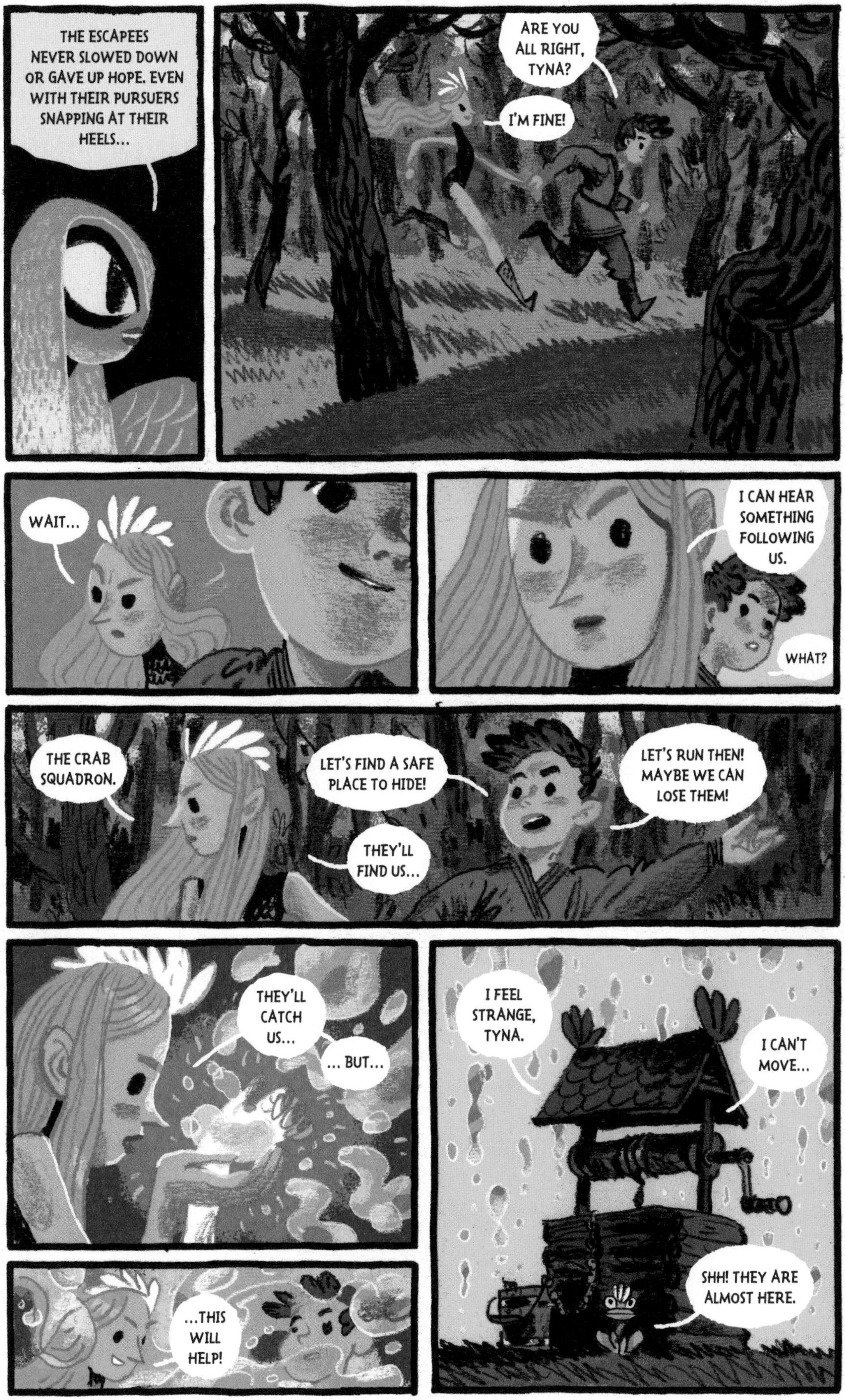
THE ESCAPEES NEVER SLOWED DOWN OR GAVE UP HOPE. EVEN WITH THEIR PURSUERS SNAPPING AT THEIR HEELS...
ARE YOU ALL RIGHT, TYNA?
I'M FINE!
WAIT...
I CAN HEAR SOMETHING FOLLOWING US.
WHAT?
THE CRAB SQUADRON.
LET'S FIND A SAFE PLACE TO HIDE!
THEY'LL FIND US...
LET'S RUN THEN! MAYBE WE CAN LOSE THEM!
THEY'LL CATCH US...
... BUT...
...THIS WILL HELP!
I FEEL STRANGE, TYNA.
I CAN'T MOVE...
SHH! THEY ARE ALMOST HERE.

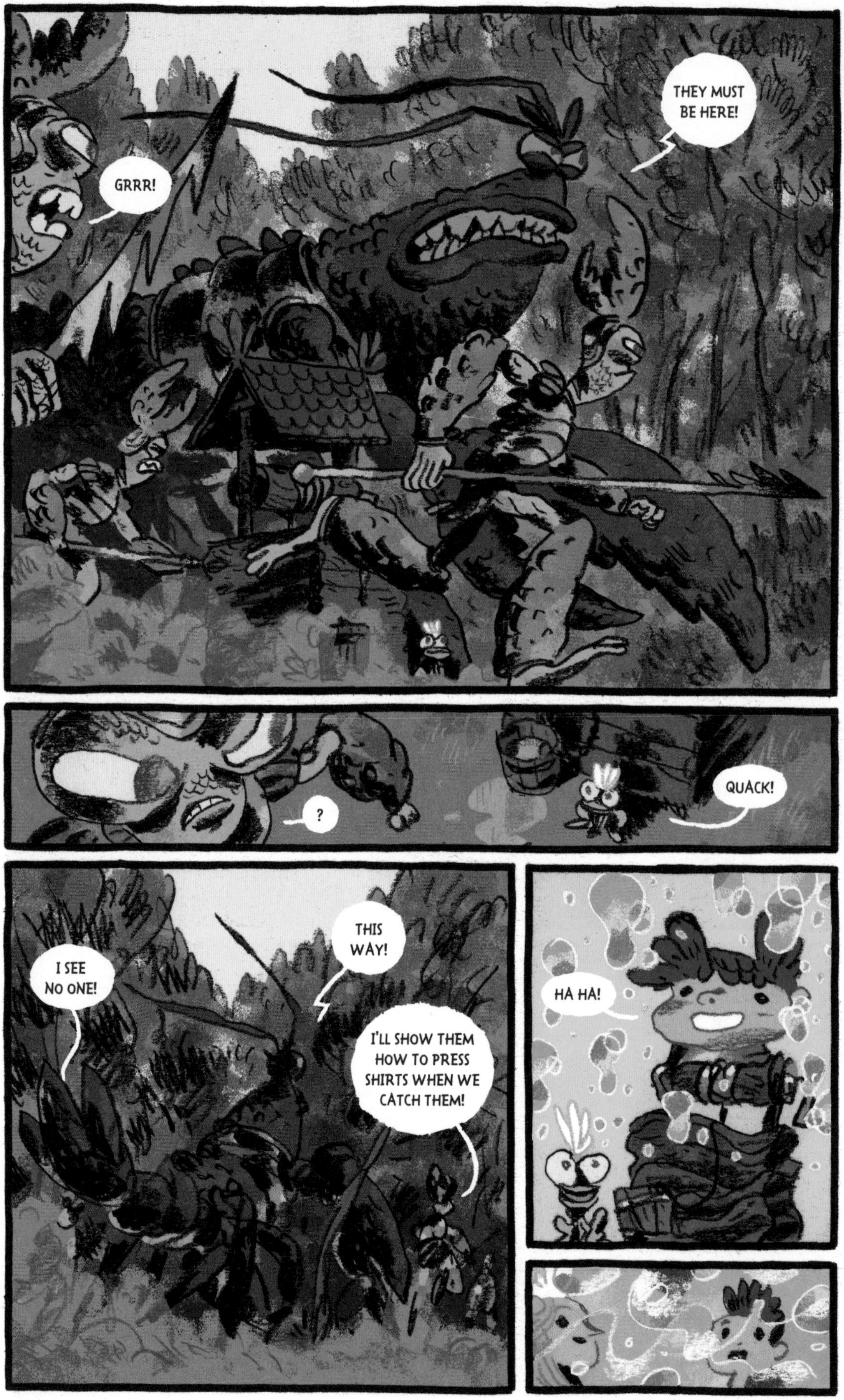
GRRR!
THEY MUST BE HERE!
?
QUACK!
I SEE NO ONE!
THIS WAY!
I'LL SHOW THEM HOW TO PRESS SHIRTS WHEN WE CATCH THEM!
HA HA!

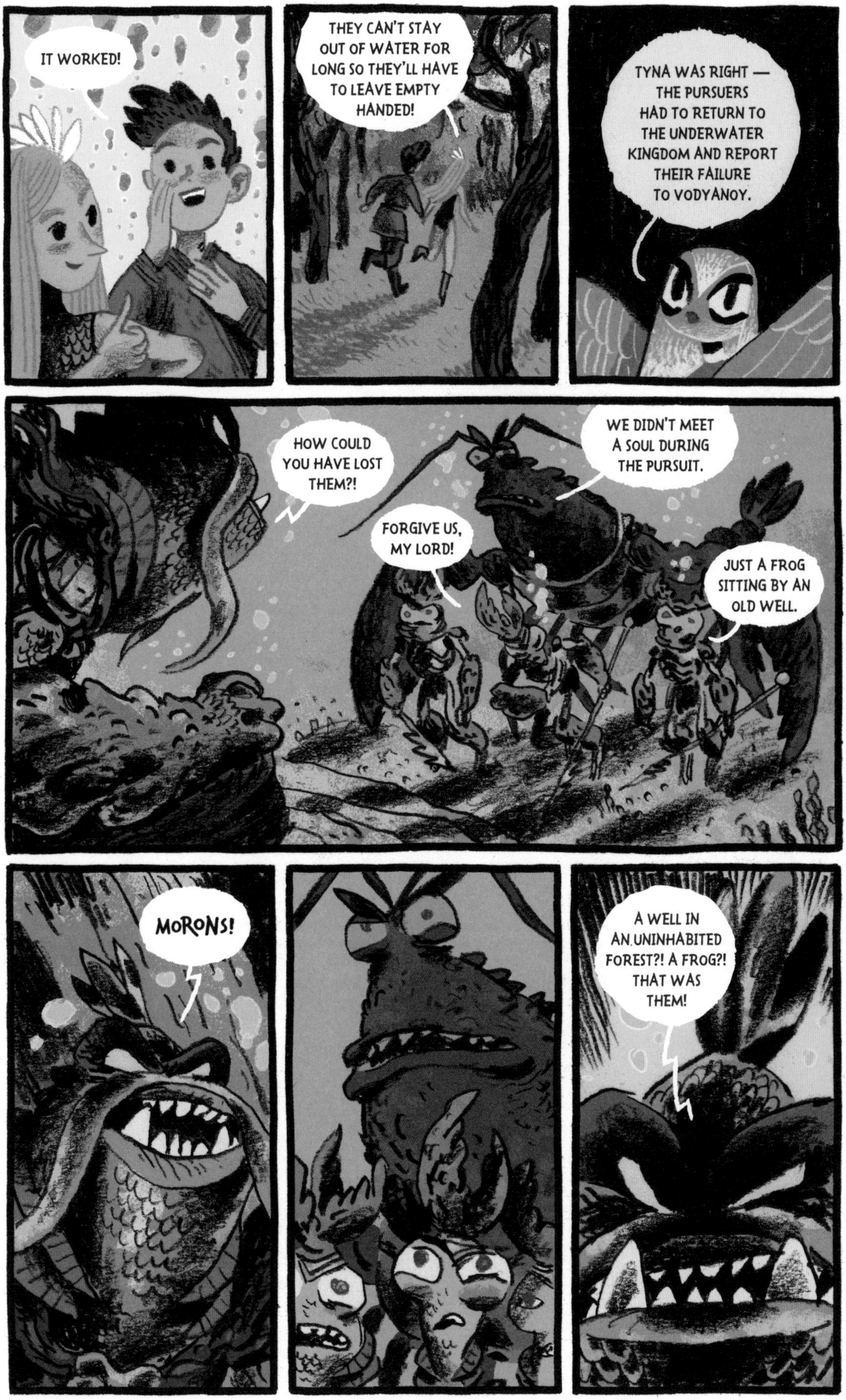
IT WORKED!
THEY CAN'T STAY OUT OF WATER FOR LONG SO THEY'LL HAVE TO LEAVE EMPTY HANDED!
TYNA WAS RIGHT — THE PURSUERS HAD TO RETURN TO THE UNDERWATER KINGDOM AND REPORT THEIR FAILURE TO VODYANOY.
HOW COULD YOU HAVE LOST THEM?!
FORGIVE US, MY LORD!
WE DIDN'T MEET A SOUL DURING THE PURSUIT.
JUST A FROG SITTING BY AN OLD WELL.
MORONS!
A WELL IN AN UNINHABITED FOREST?! A FROG?! THAT WAS THEM!

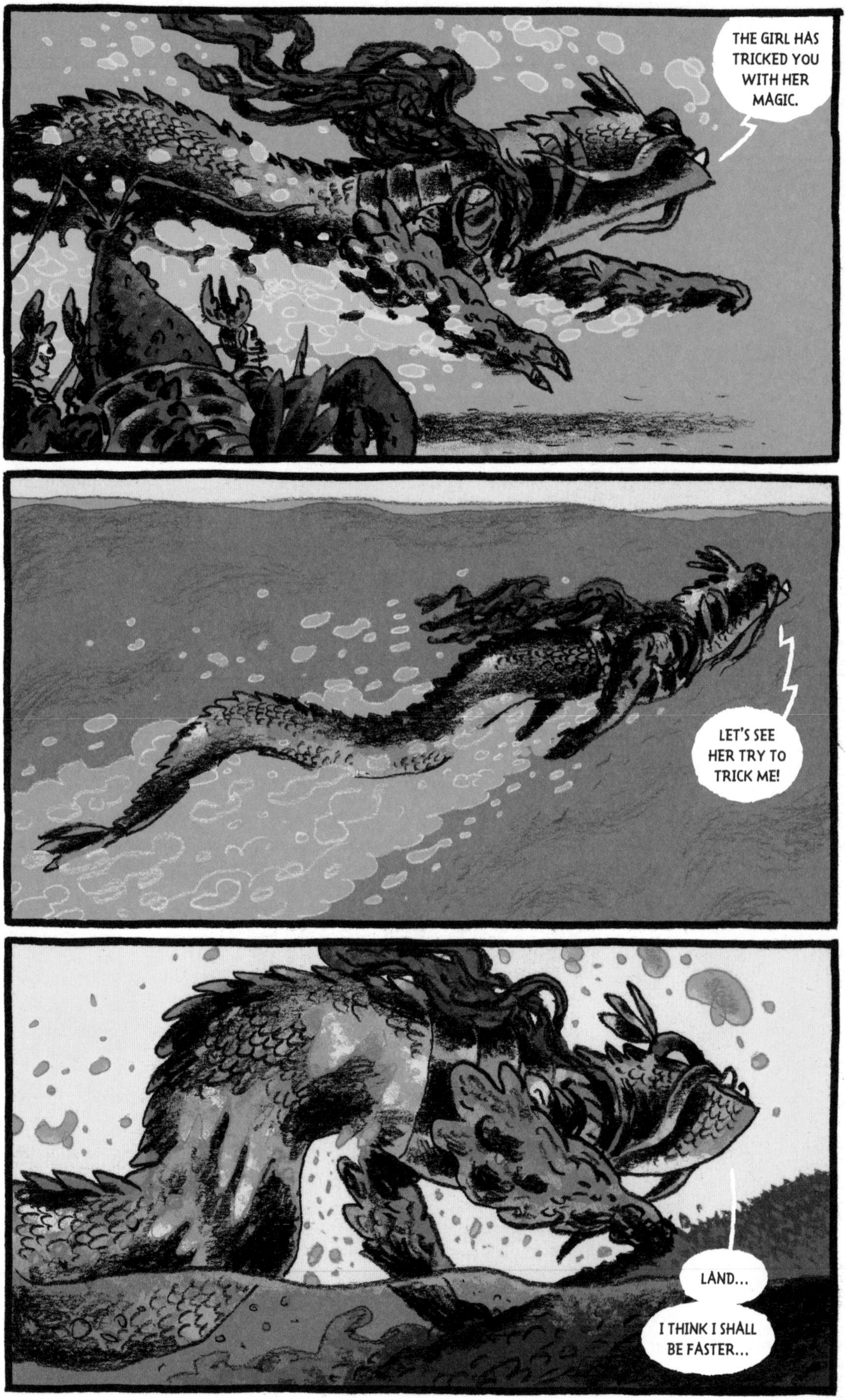
THE GIRL HAS TRICKED YOU WITH HER MAGIC.
LET'S SEE HER TRY TO TRICK ME!
LAND...
I THINK I SHALL BE FASTER...

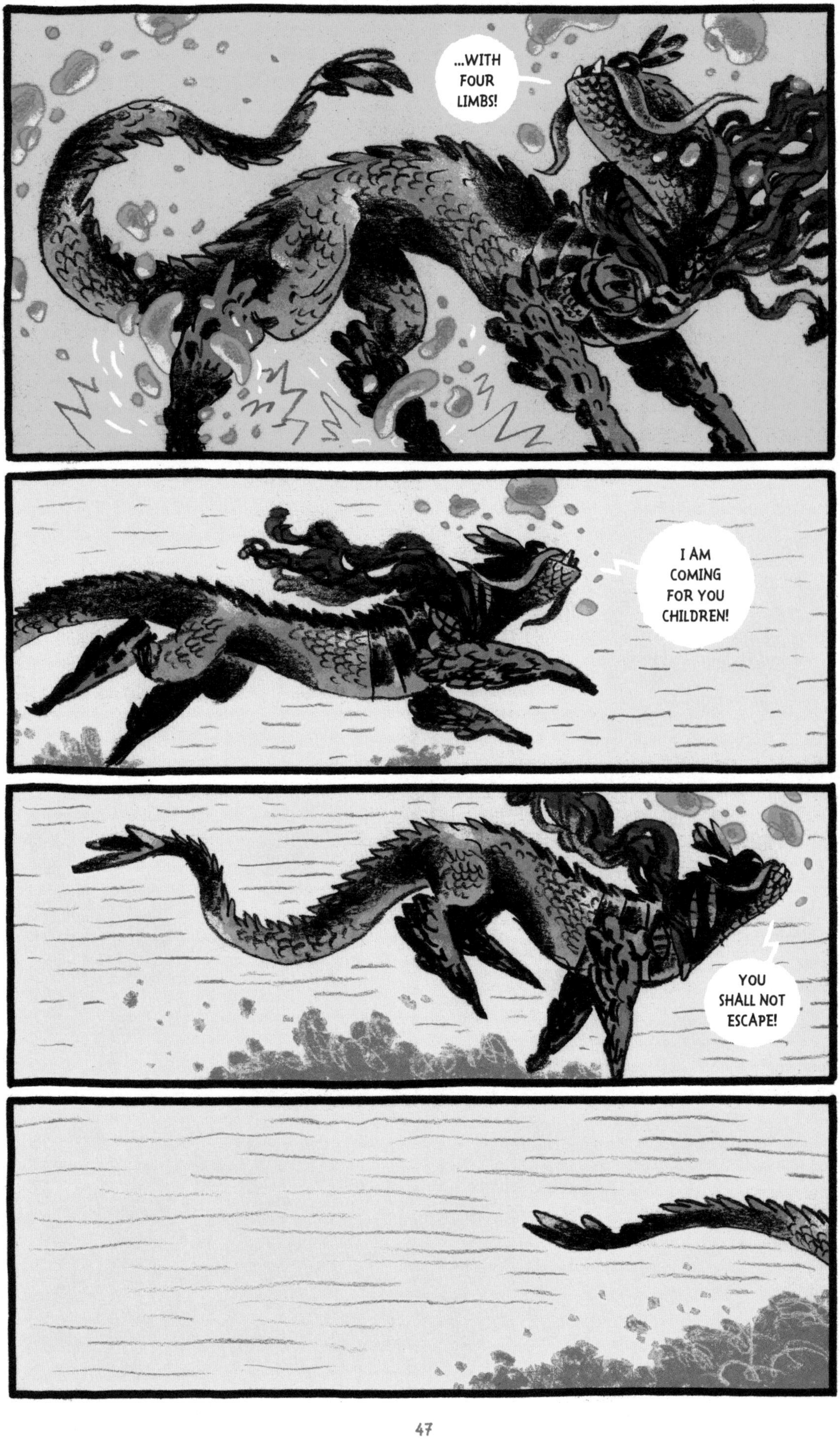
...WITH FOUR LIMBS!
I AM COMING FOR YOU CHILDREN!
YOU SHALL NOT ESCAPE!

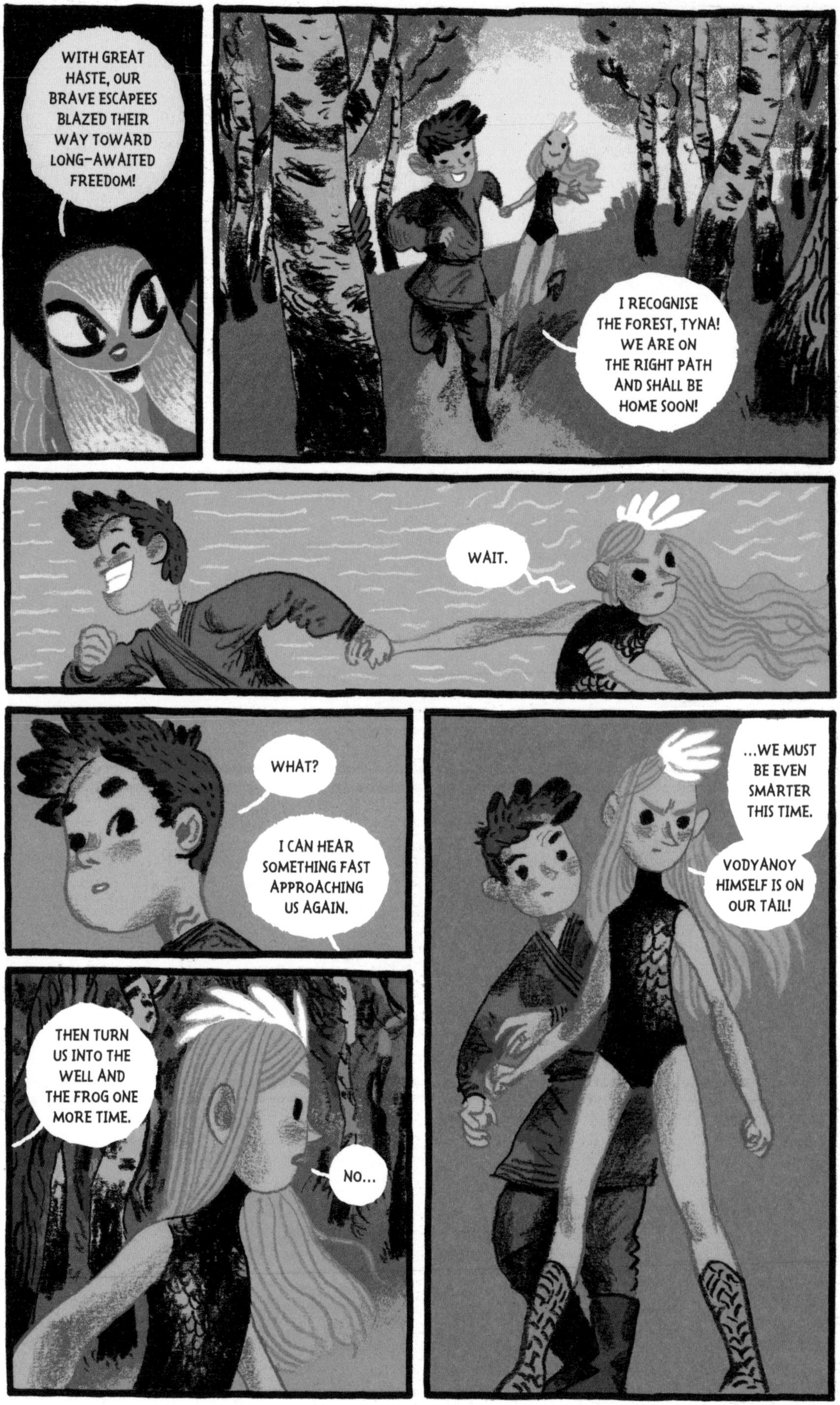
WITH GREAT HASTE, OUR BRAVE ESCAPEES BLAZED THEIR WAY TOWARD LONG-AWAITED FREEDOM!
I RECOGNISE THE FOREST, TYNA! WE ARE ON THE RIGHT PATH AND SHALL BE HOME SOON!
WAIT.
WHAT?
I CAN HEAR SOMETHING FAST APPROACHING US AGAIN.
THEN TURN US INTO THE WELL AND THE FROG ONE MORE TIME.
NO...
...WE MUST BE EVEN SMARTER THIS TIME.
VODYANOY HIMSELF IS ON OUR TAIL!

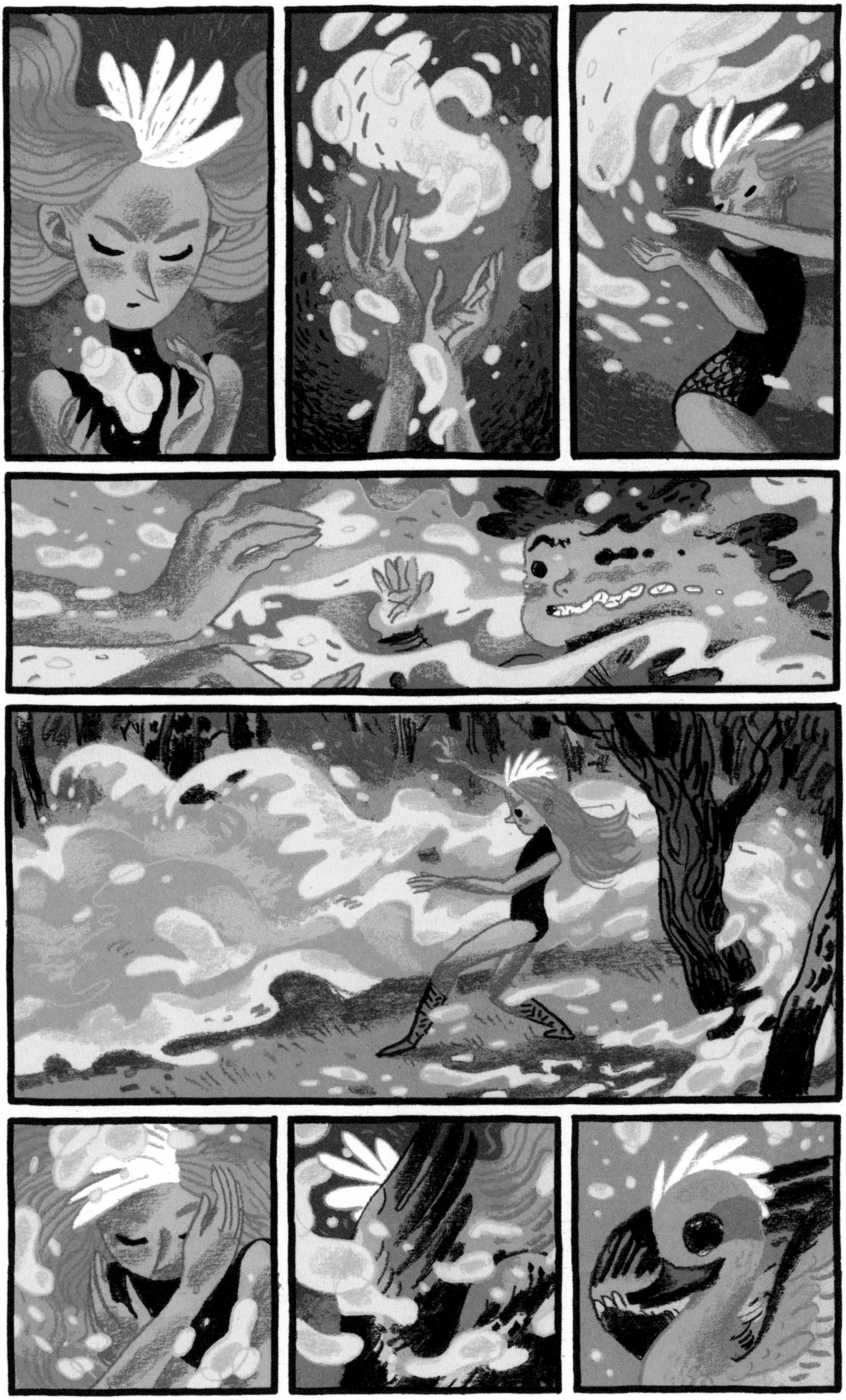

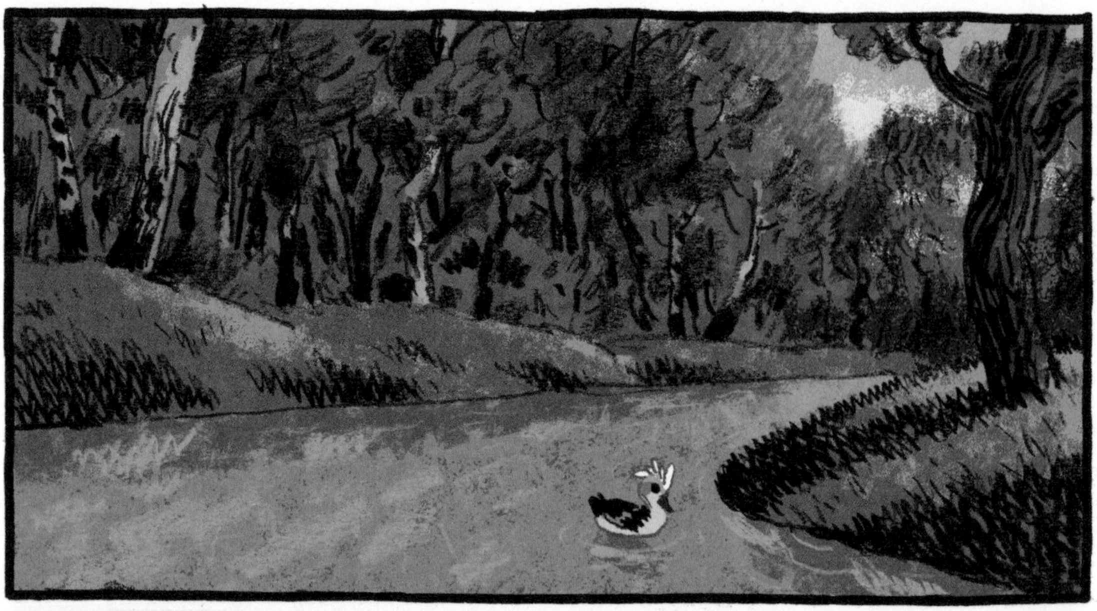

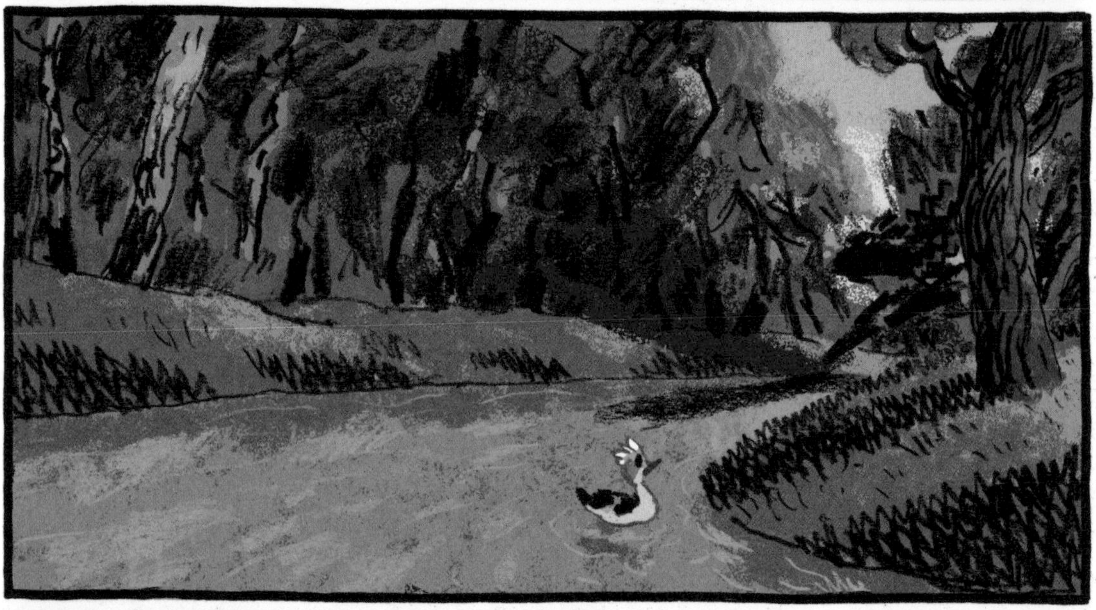

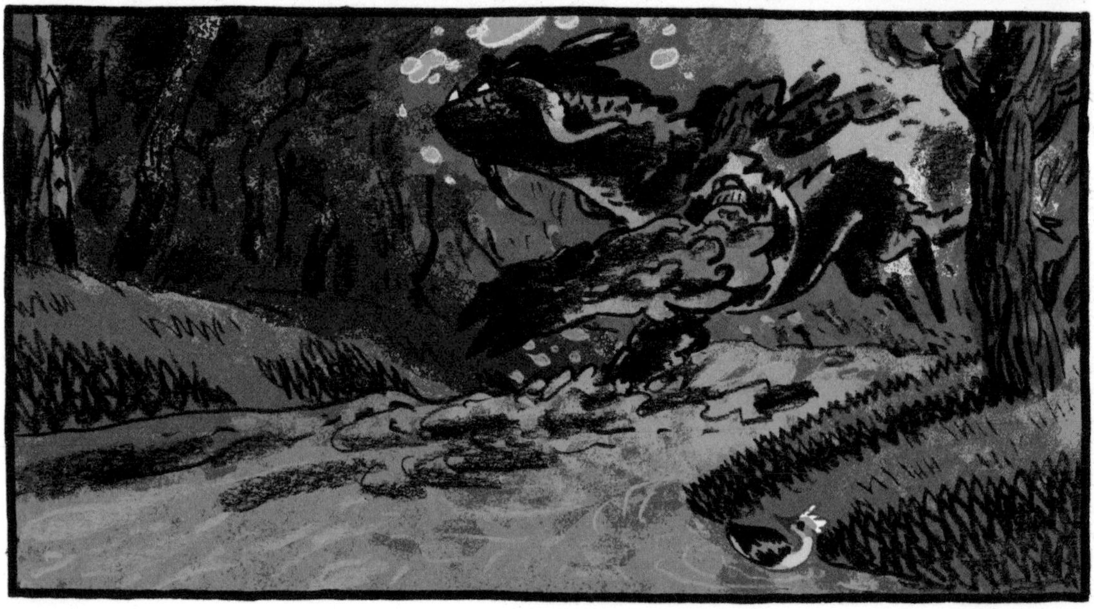

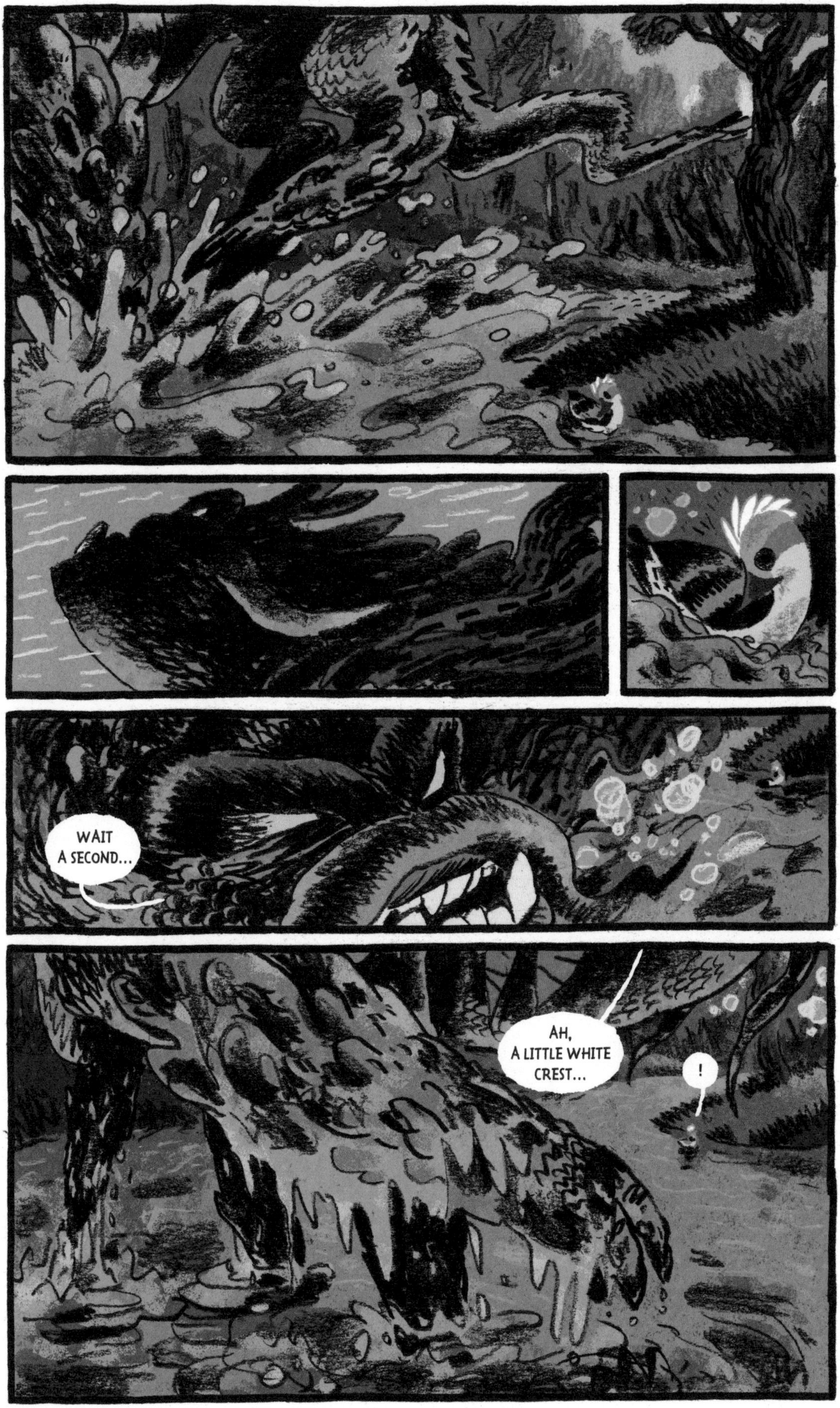
WAIT A SECOND...
AH, A LITTLE WHITE CREST...
!

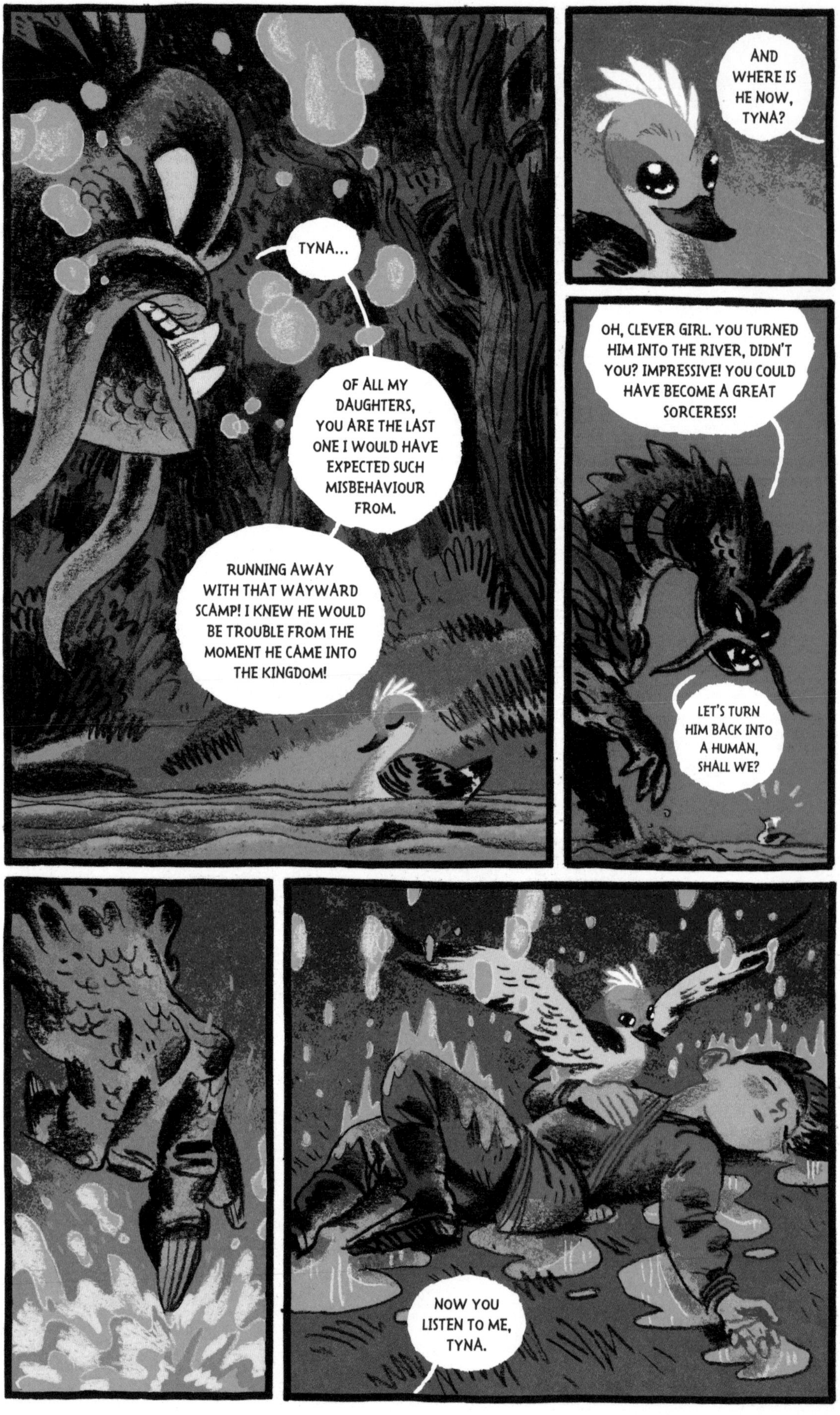
TYNA...
OF ALL MY DAUGHTERS, YOU ARE THE LAST ONE I WOULD HAVE EXPECTED SUCH MISBEHAVIOUR FROM.
RUNNING AWAY WITH THAT WAYWARD SCAMP! I KNEW HE WOULD BE TROUBLE FROM THE MOMENT HE CAME INTO THE KINGDOM!
AND WHERE IS HE NOW, TYNA?
OH, CLEVER GIRL. YOU TURNED HIM INTO THE RIVER, DIDN'T YOU? IMPRESSIVE! YOU COULD HAVE BECOME A GREAT SORCERESS!
LET'S TURN HIM BACK INTO A HUMAN, SHALL WE?
NOW YOU LISTEN TO ME, TYNA.

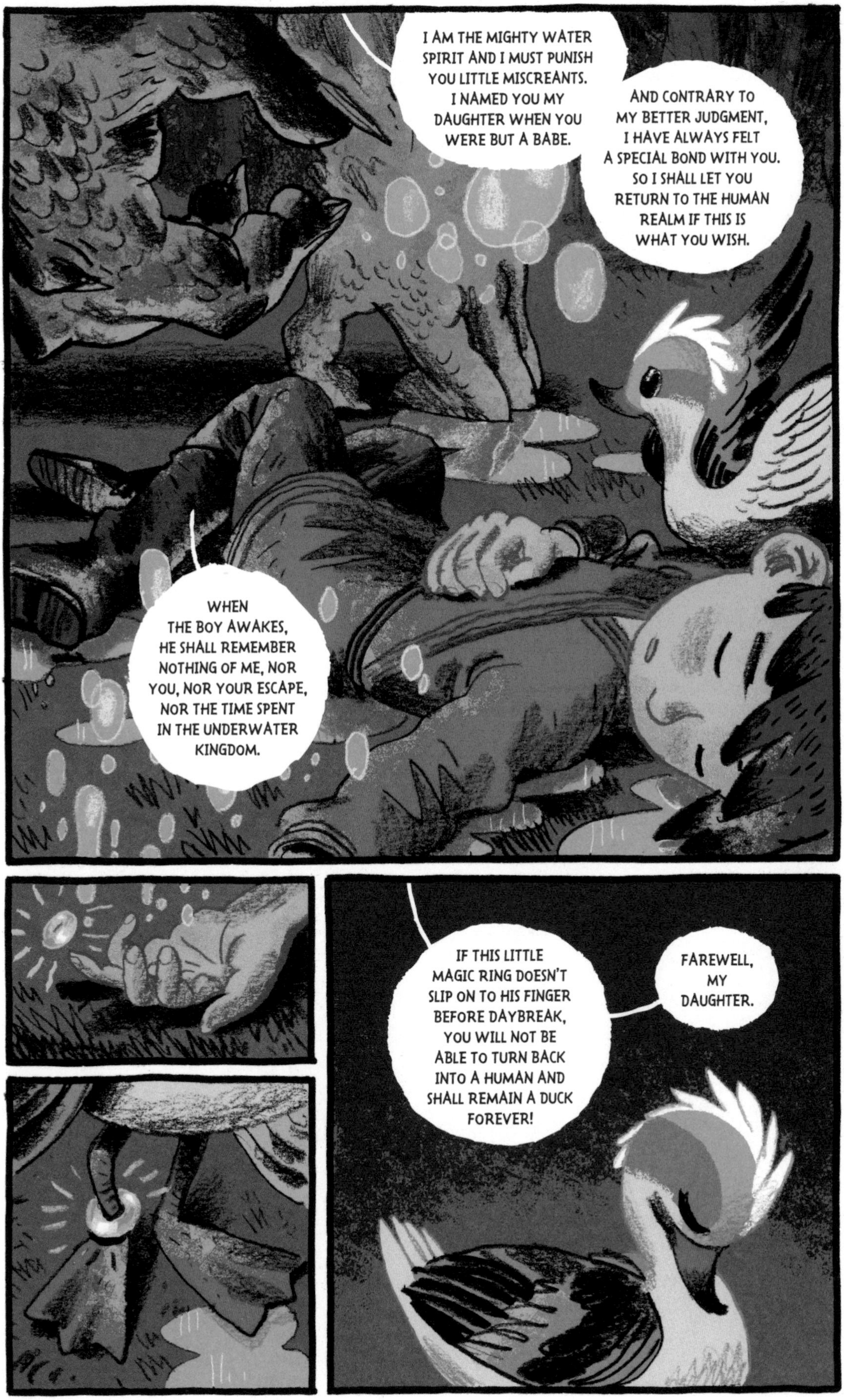
I AM THE MIGHTY WATER SPIRIT AND I MUST PUNISH YOU LITTLE MISCREANTS. I NAMED YOU MY DAUGHTER WHEN YOU WERE BUT A BABE.
AND CONTRARY TO MY BETTER JUDGMENT, I HAVE ALWAYS FELT A SPECIAL BOND WITH YOU. SO I SHALL LET YOU RETURN TO THE HUMAN REALM IF THIS IS WHAT YOU WISH.
WHEN THE BOY AWAKES, HE SHALL REMEMBER NOTHING OF ME, NOR YOU, NOR YOUR ESCAPE, NOR THE TIME SPENT IN THE UNDERWATER KINGDOM.
IF THIS LITTLE MAGIC RING DOESN'T SLIP ON TO HIS FINGER BEFORE DAYBREAK, YOU WILL NOT BE ABLE TO TURN BACK INTO A HUMAN AND SHALL REMAIN A DUCK FOREVER!
FAREWELL, MY DAUGHTER.

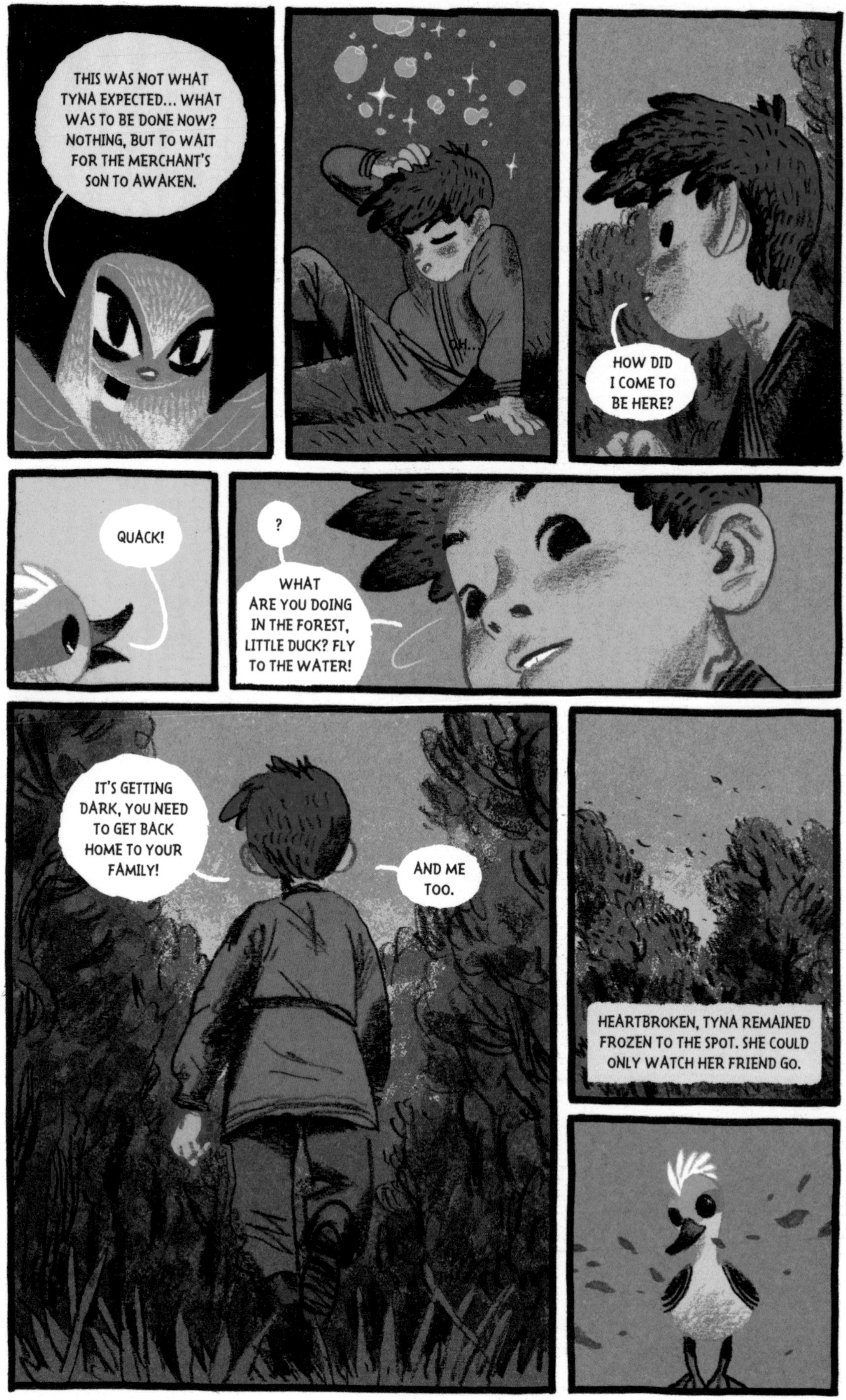
THIS WAS NOT WHAT TYNA EXPECTED... WHAT WAS TO BE DONE NOW? NOTHING, BUT TO WAIT FOR THE MERCHANT'S SON TO AWAKEN.
OH...
HOW DID I COME TO BE HERE?
QUACK!
?
WHAT ARE YOU DOING IN THE FOREST, LITTLE DUCK? FLY TO THE WATER!
IT'S GETTING DARK, YOU NEED TO GET BACK HOME TO YOUR FAMILY!
AND ME TOO.
HEARTBROKEN, TYNA REMAINED FROZEN TO THE SPOT. SHE COULD ONLY WATCH HER FRIEND GO.

HOME AT LAST

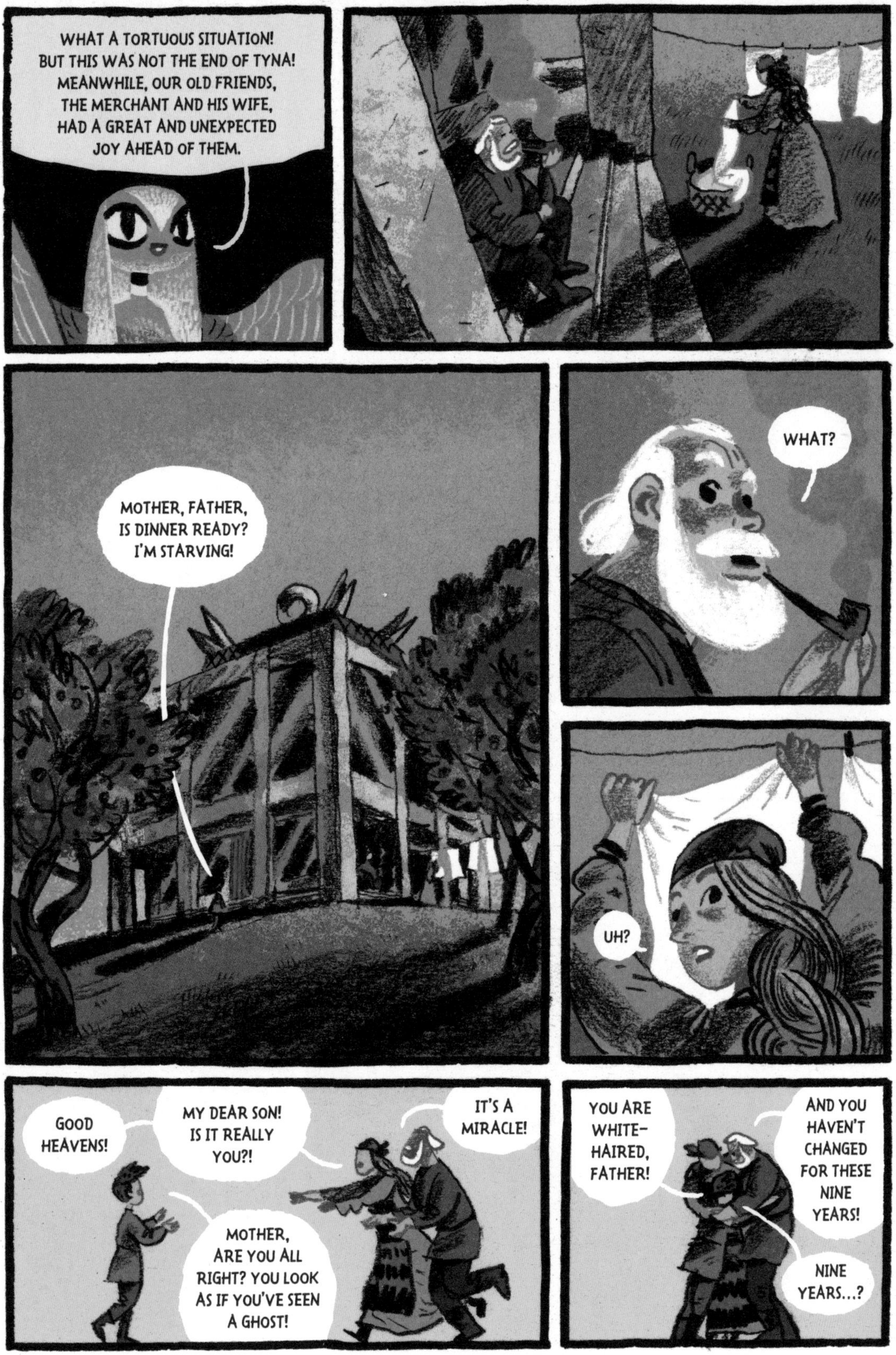
WHAT A TORTUOUS SITUATION! BUT THIS WAS NOT THE END OF TYNA! MEANWHILE, OUR OLD FRIENDS, THE MERCHANT AND HIS WIFE, HAD A GREAT AND UNEXPECTED JOY AHEAD OF THEM.
MOTHER, FATHER, IS DINNER READY? I'M STARVING!
WHAT?
UH?
GOOD HEAVENS!
MY DEAR SON! IS IT REALLY YOU?!
IT'S A MIRACLE!
MOTHER, ARE YOU ALL RIGHT? YOU LOOK AS IF YOU'VE SEEN A GHOST!
YOU ARE WHITE-HAIRED, FATHER!
AND YOU HAVEN'T CHANGED FOR THESE NINE YEARS!
NINE YEARS...?

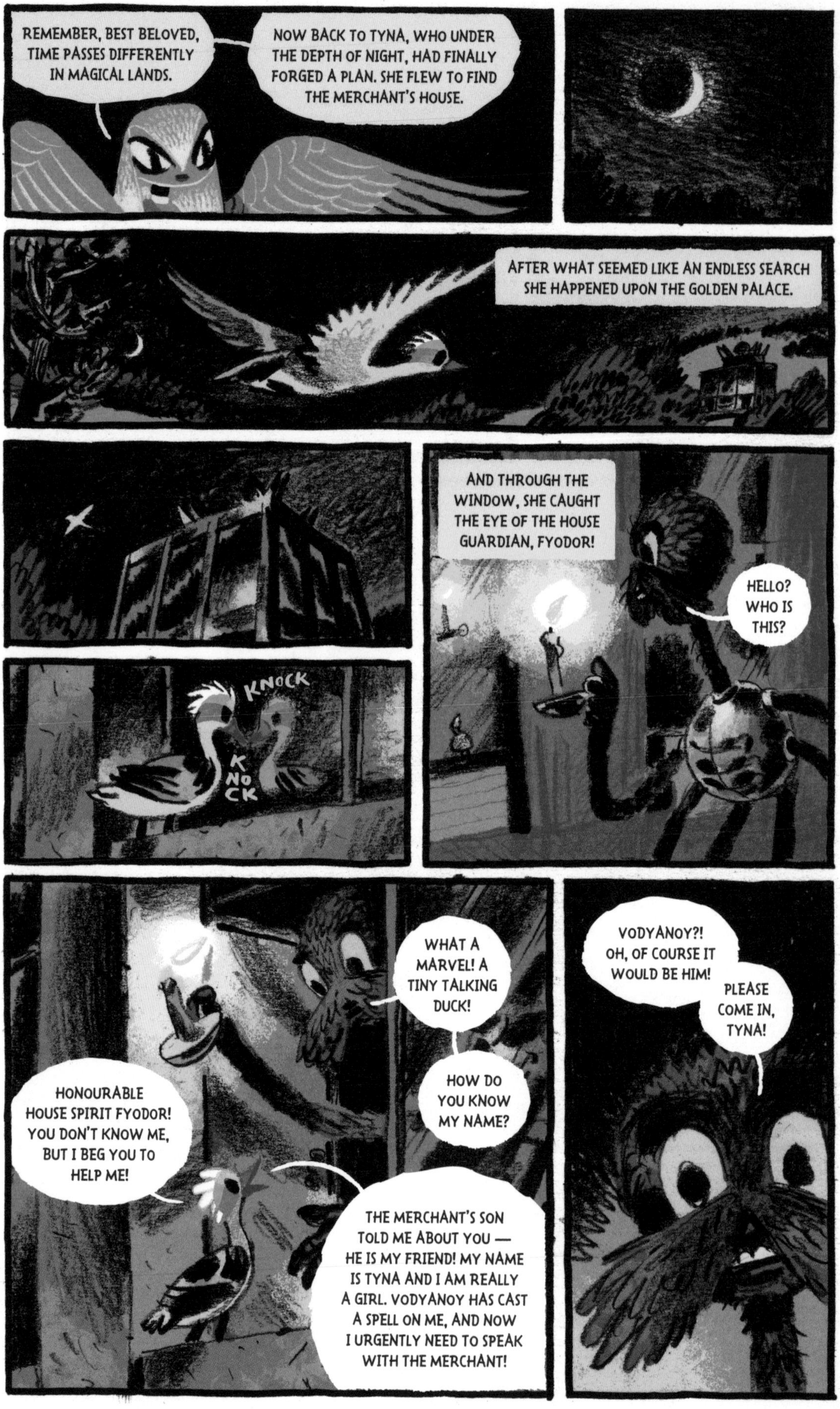
REMEMBER, BEST BELOVED, TIME PASSES DIFFERENTLY IN MAGICAL LANDS.
NOW BACK TO TYNA, WHO UNDER THE DEPTH OF NIGHT, HAD FINALLY FORGED A PLAN. SHE FLEW TO FIND THE MERCHANT'S HOUSE.
AFTER WHAT SEEMED LIKE AN ENDLESS SEARCH SHE HAPPENED UPON THE GOLDEN PALACE.
KNOCK
KNOCK
AND THROUGH THE WINDOW, SHE CAUGHT THE EYE OF THE HOUSE GUARDIAN, FYODOR!
HELLO? WHO IS THIS?
WHAT A MARVEL! A TINY TALKING DUCK!
HOW DO YOU KNOW MY NAME?
HONOURABLE HOUSE SPIRIT FYODOR! YOU DON'T KNOW ME, BUT I BEG YOU TO HELP ME!
THE MERCHANT'S SON TOLD ME ABOUT YOU — HE IS MY FRIEND! MY NAME IS TYNA AND I AM REALLY A GIRL. VODYANOY HAS CAST A SPELL ON ME, AND NOW I URGENTLY NEED TO SPEAK WITH THE MERCHANT!
VODYANOY?! OH, OF COURSE IT WOULD BE HIM!
PLEASE COME IN, TYNA!

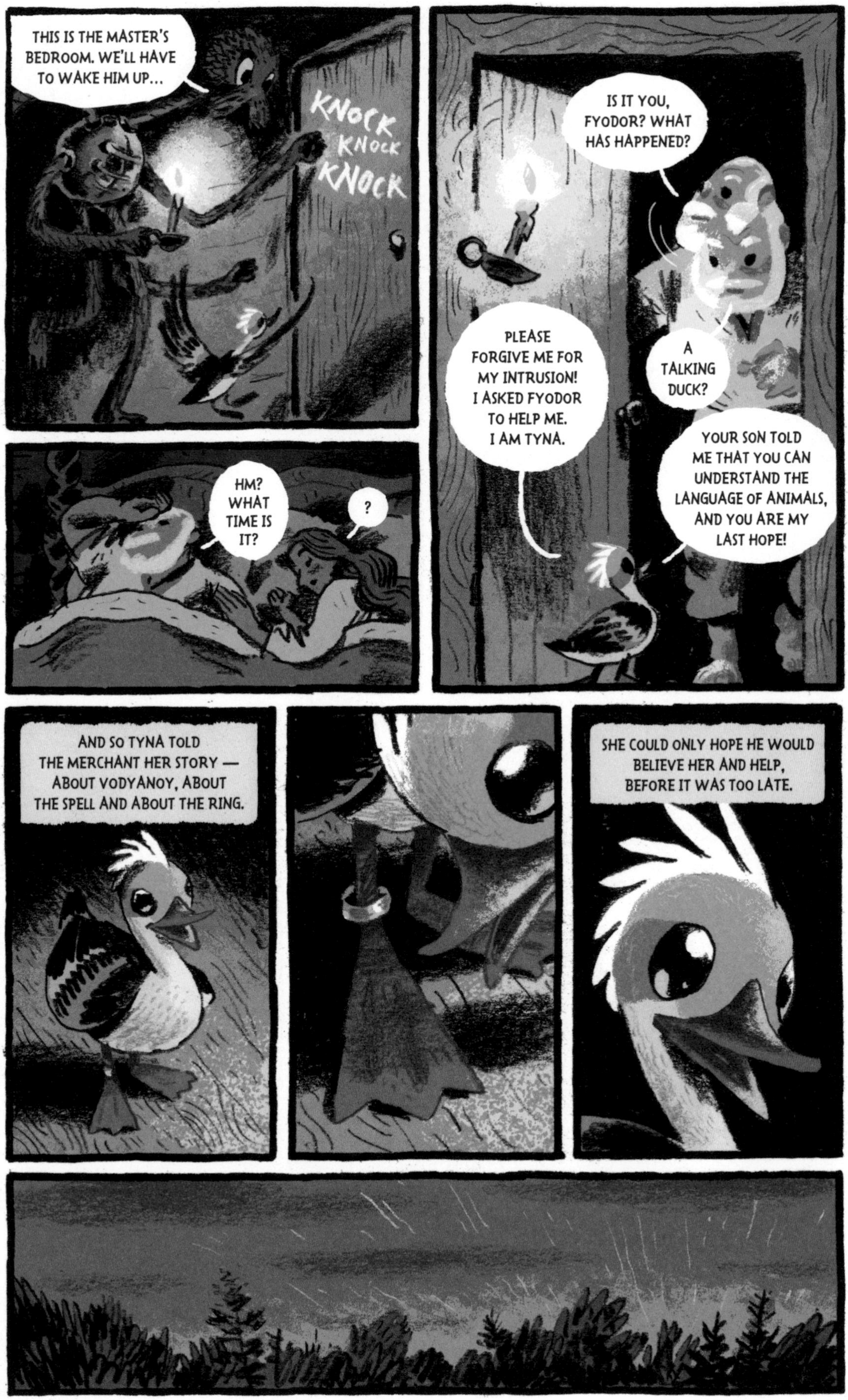
THIS IS THE MASTER'S BEDROOM. WE'LL HAVE TO WAKE HIM UP...
KNOCK KNOCK KNOCK
HM? WHAT TIME IS IT?
?
IS IT YOU, FYODOR? WHAT HAS HAPPENED?
PLEASE FORGIVE ME FOR MY INTRUSION! I ASKED FYODOR TO HELP ME. I AM TYNA.
A TALKING DUCK?
YOUR SON TOLD ME THAT YOU CAN UNDERSTAND THE LANGUAGE OF ANIMALS, AND YOU ARE MY LAST HOPE!
AND SO TYNA TOLD THE MERCHANT HER STORY — ABOUT VODYANOY, ABOUT THE SPELL AND ABOUT THE RING.
SHE COULD ONLY HOPE HE WOULD BELIEVE HER AND HELP, BEFORE IT WAS TOO LATE.

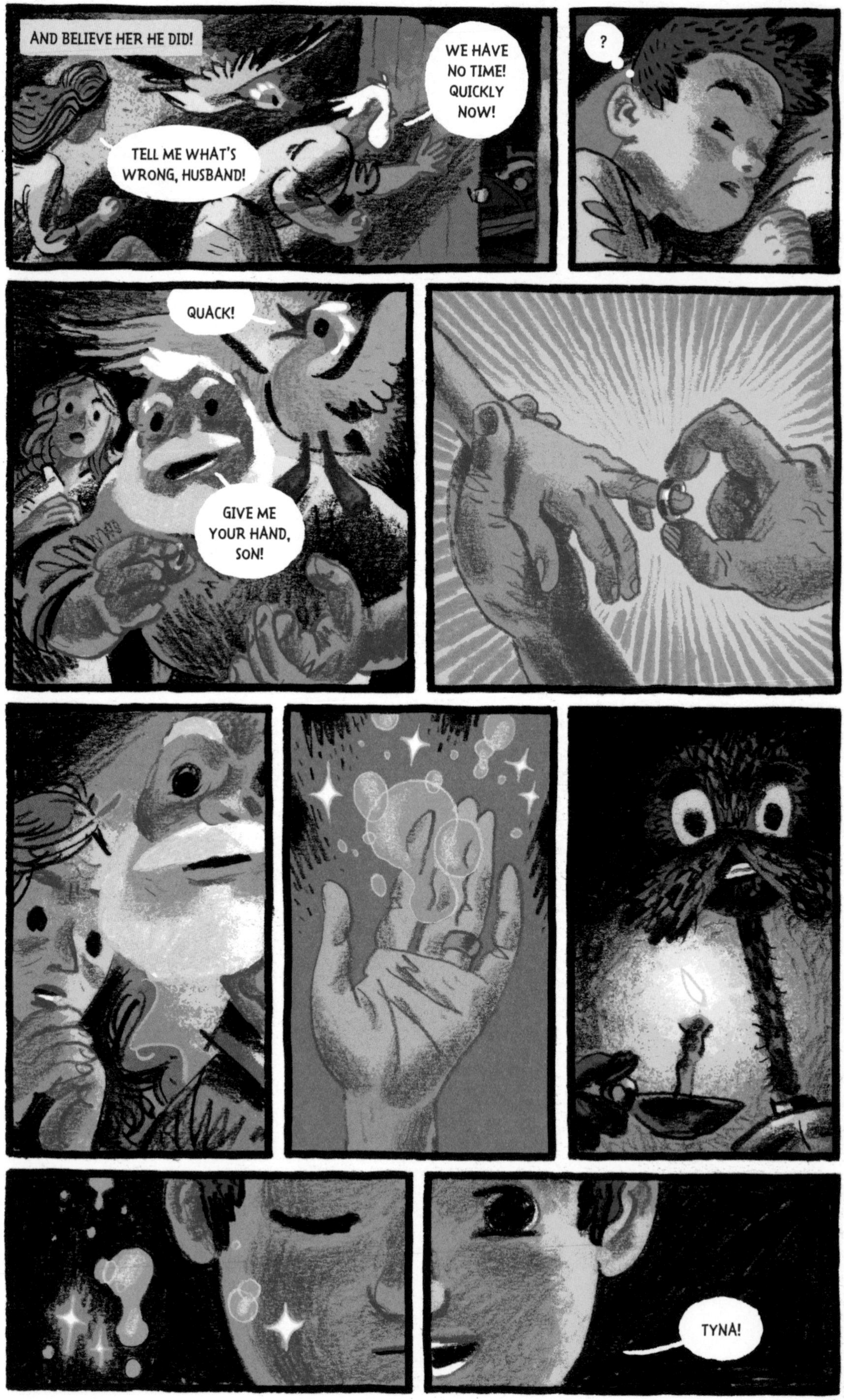
AND BELIEVE HER HE DID!
WE HAVE NO TIME! QUICKLY NOW!
TELL ME WHAT'S WRONG, HUSBAND!
?
QUACK!
GIVE ME YOUR HAND, SON!
TYNA!

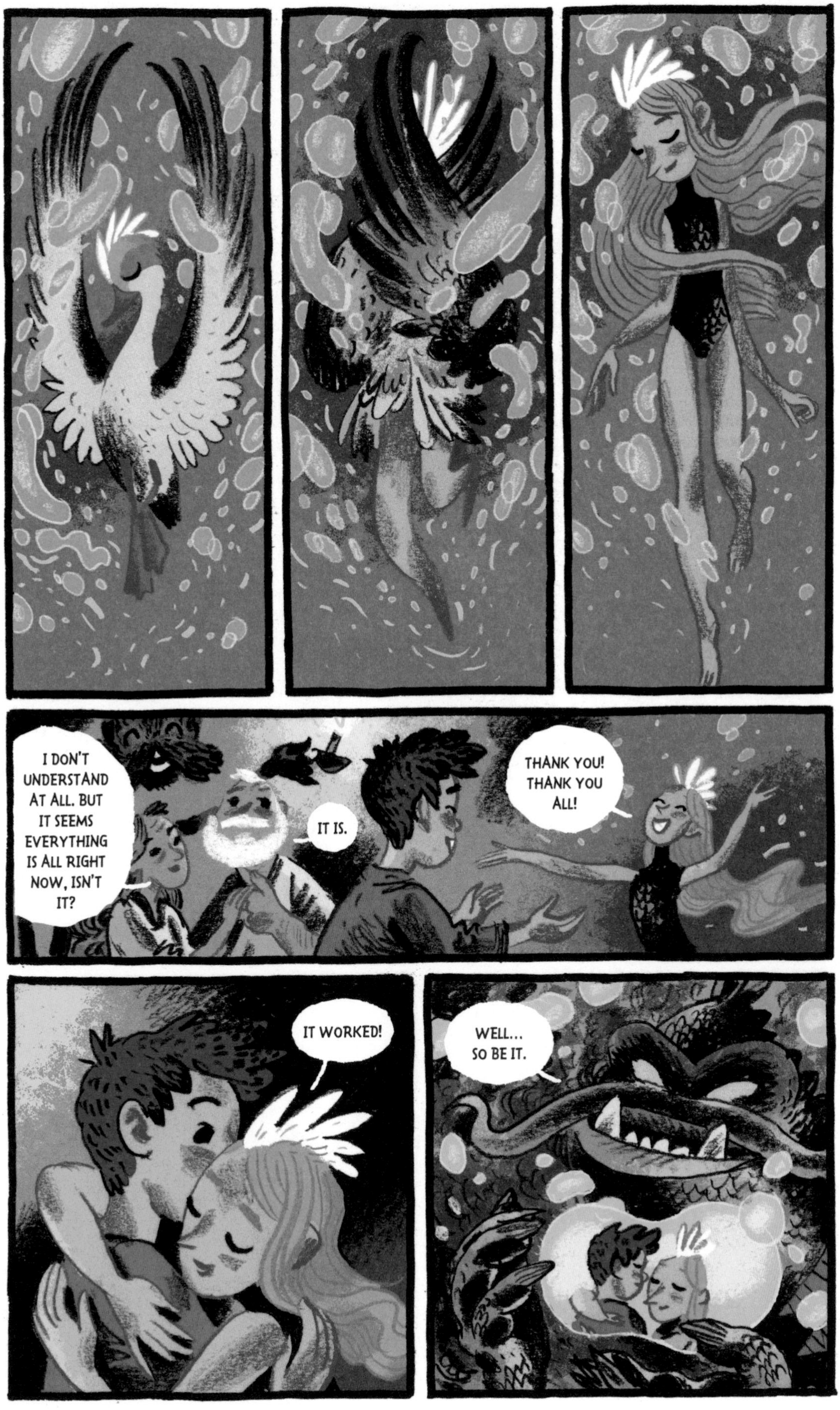
I DON'T UNDERSTAND AT ALL. BUT IT SEEMS EVERYTHING IS ALL RIGHT NOW, ISN'T IT?
IT IS.
THANK YOU! THANK YOU ALL!
IT WORKED!
WELL... SO BE IT.

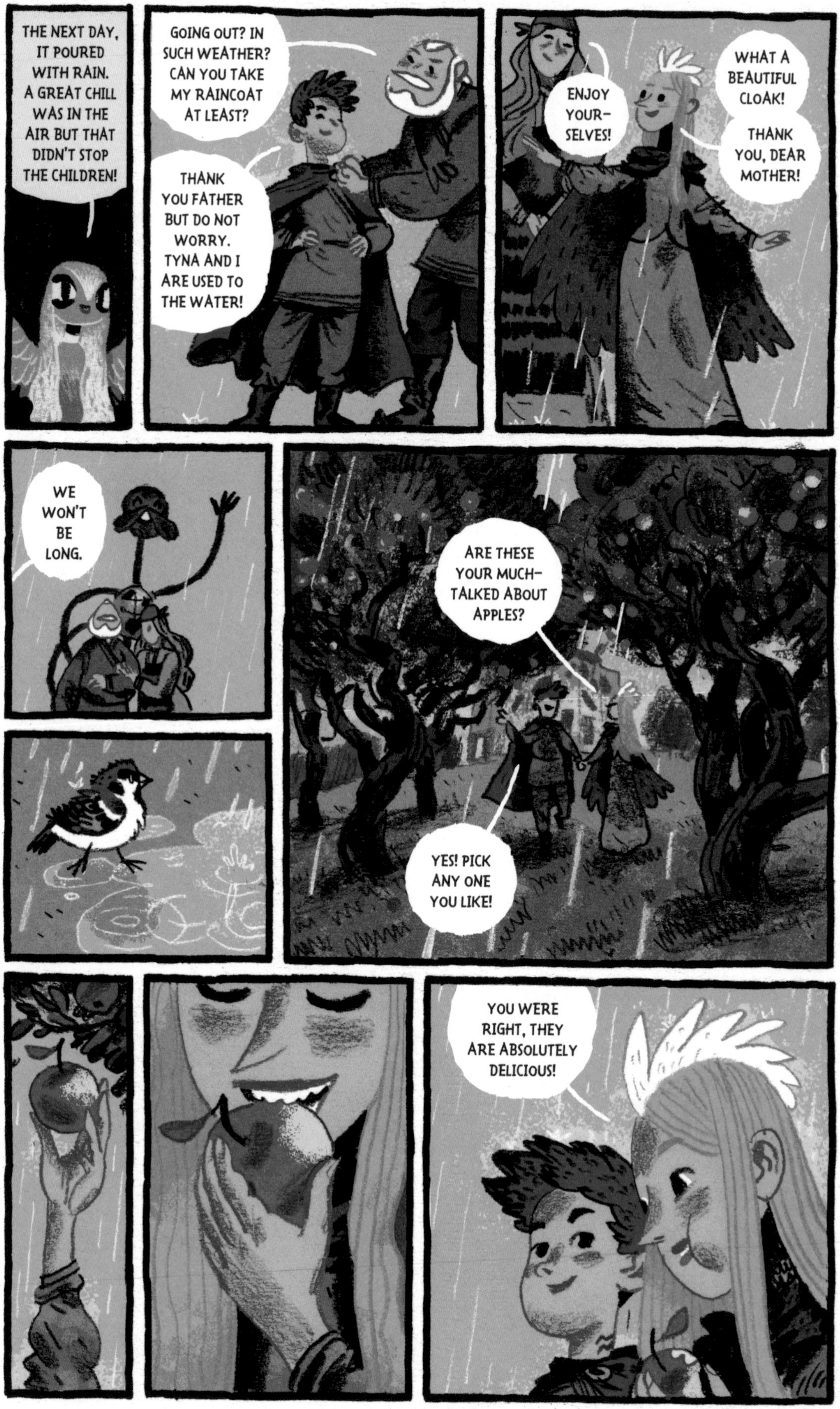
THE NEXT DAY, IT POURED WITH RAIN. A GREAT CHILL WAS IN THE AIR BUT THAT DIDN'T STOP THE CHILDREN!
GOING OUT? IN SUCH WEATHER? CAN YOU TAKE MY RAINCOAT AT LEAST?
THANK YOU FATHER BUT DO NOT WORRY. TYNA AND I ARE USED TO THE WATER!
ENJOY YOUR-SELVES!
WHAT A BEAUTIFUL CLOAK!
THANK YOU, DEAR MOTHER!
WE WON'T BE LONG.
ARE THESE YOUR MUCH-TALKED ABOUT APPLES?
YES! PICK ANY ONE YOU LIKE!
YOU WERE RIGHT, THEY ARE ABSOLUTELY DELICIOUS!

TYNA

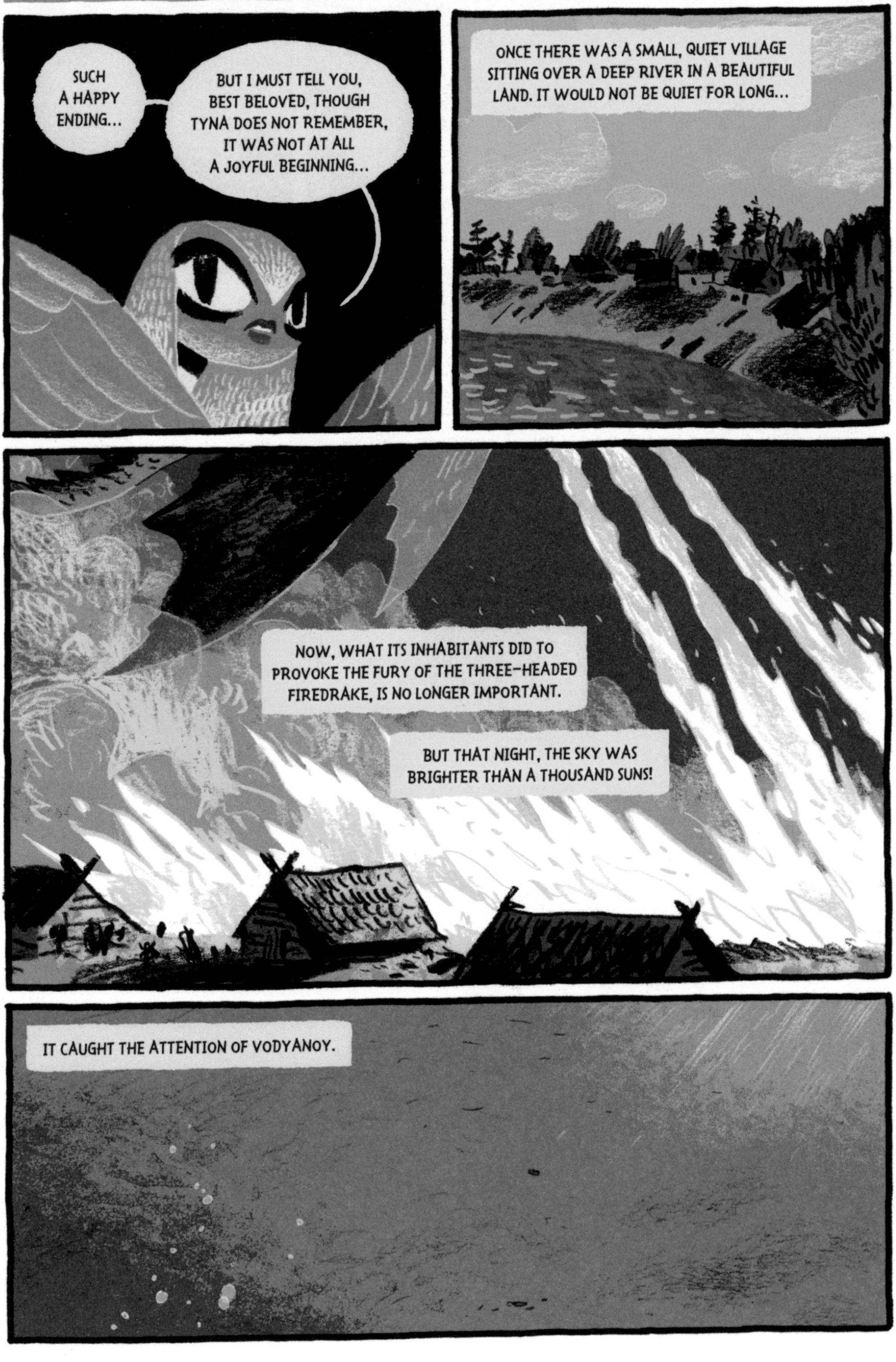
SUCH A HAPPY ENDING...
BUT I MUST TELL YOU, BEST BELOVED, THOUGH TYNA DOES NOT REMEMBER, IT WAS NOT AT ALL A JOYFUL BEGINNING...
ONCE THERE WAS A SMALL, QUIET VILLAGE SITTING OVER A DEEP RIVER IN A BEAUTIFUL LAND. IT WOULD NOT BE QUIET FOR LONG...
NOW, WHAT ITS INHABITANTS DID TO PROVOKE THE FURY OF THE THREE-HEADED FIREDRAKE, IS NO LONGER IMPORTANT.
BUT THAT NIGHT, THE SKY WAS BRIGHTER THAN A THOUSAND SUNS!
IT CAUGHT THE ATTENTION OF VODYANOY.

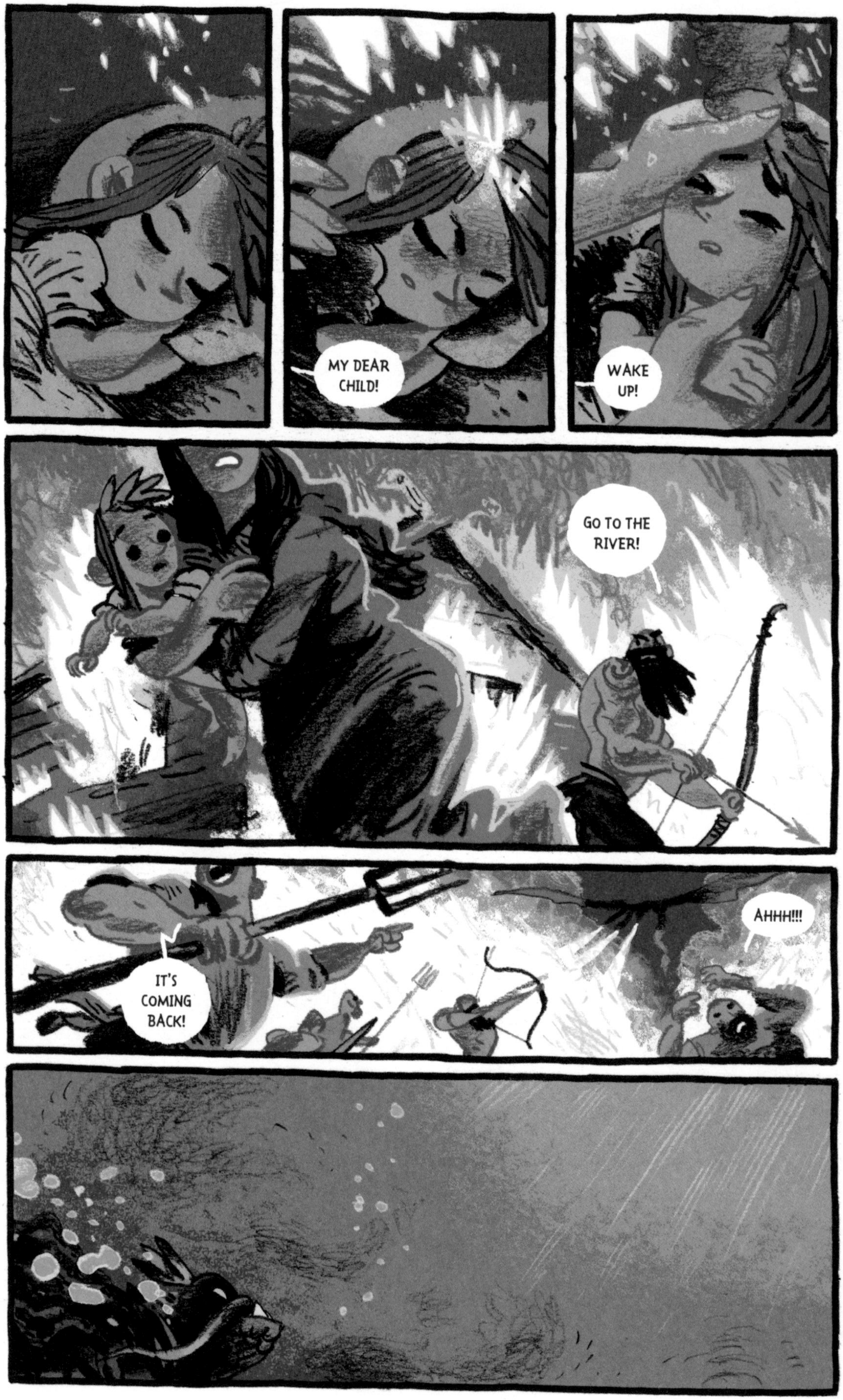
MY DEAR CHILD!
WAKE UP!
GO TO THE RIVER!
IT'S COMING BACK!
AHHH!!!

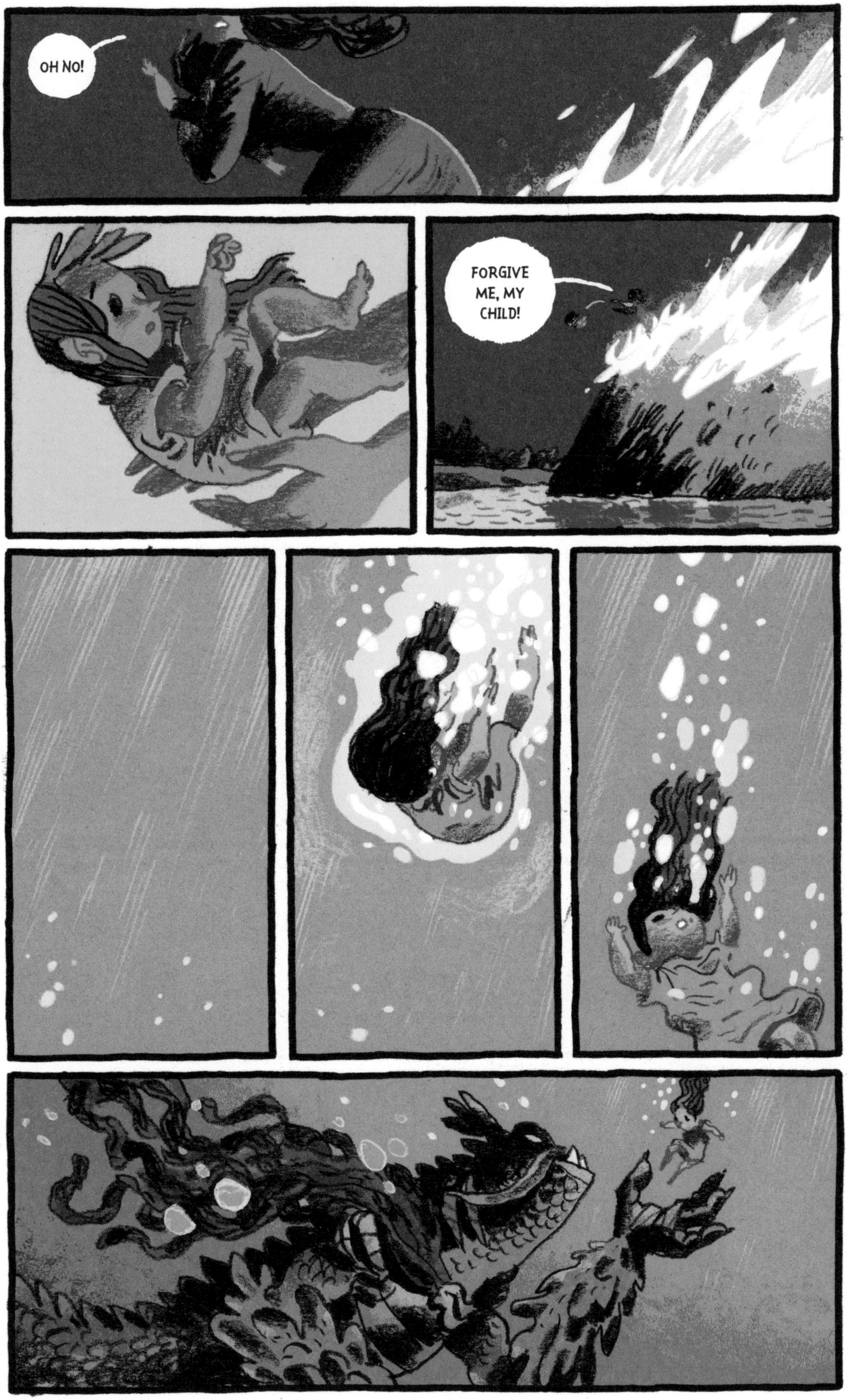
OH NO!
FORGIVE ME, MY CHILD!

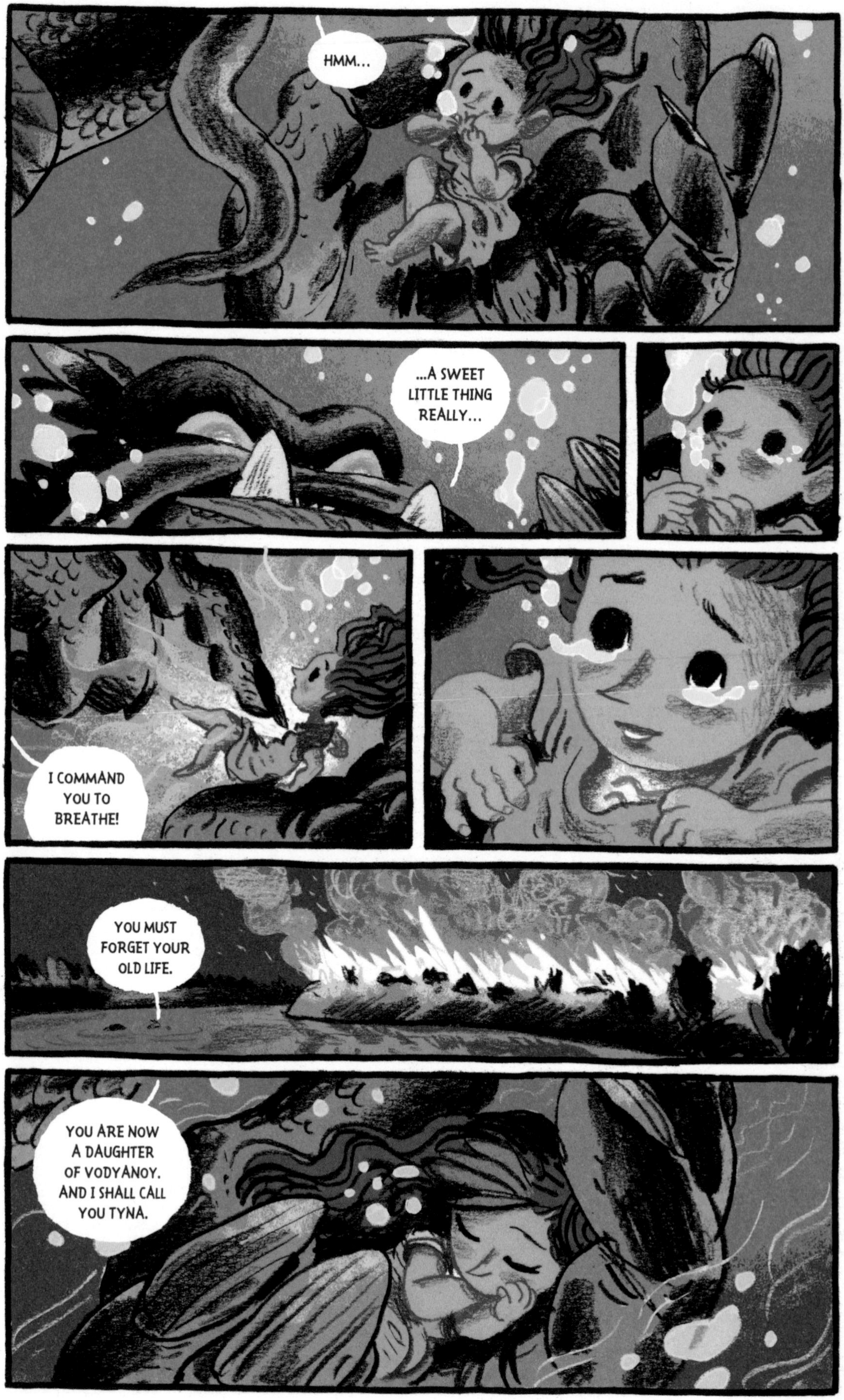
HMM...
...A SWEET LITTLE THING REALLY...
I COMMAND YOU TO BREATHE!
YOU MUST FORGET YOUR OLD LIFE.
YOU ARE NOW A DAUGHTER OF VODYANOY. AND I SHALL CALL YOU TYNA.

BRAND NEW ADVENTURES IN THE

COMING SOON!

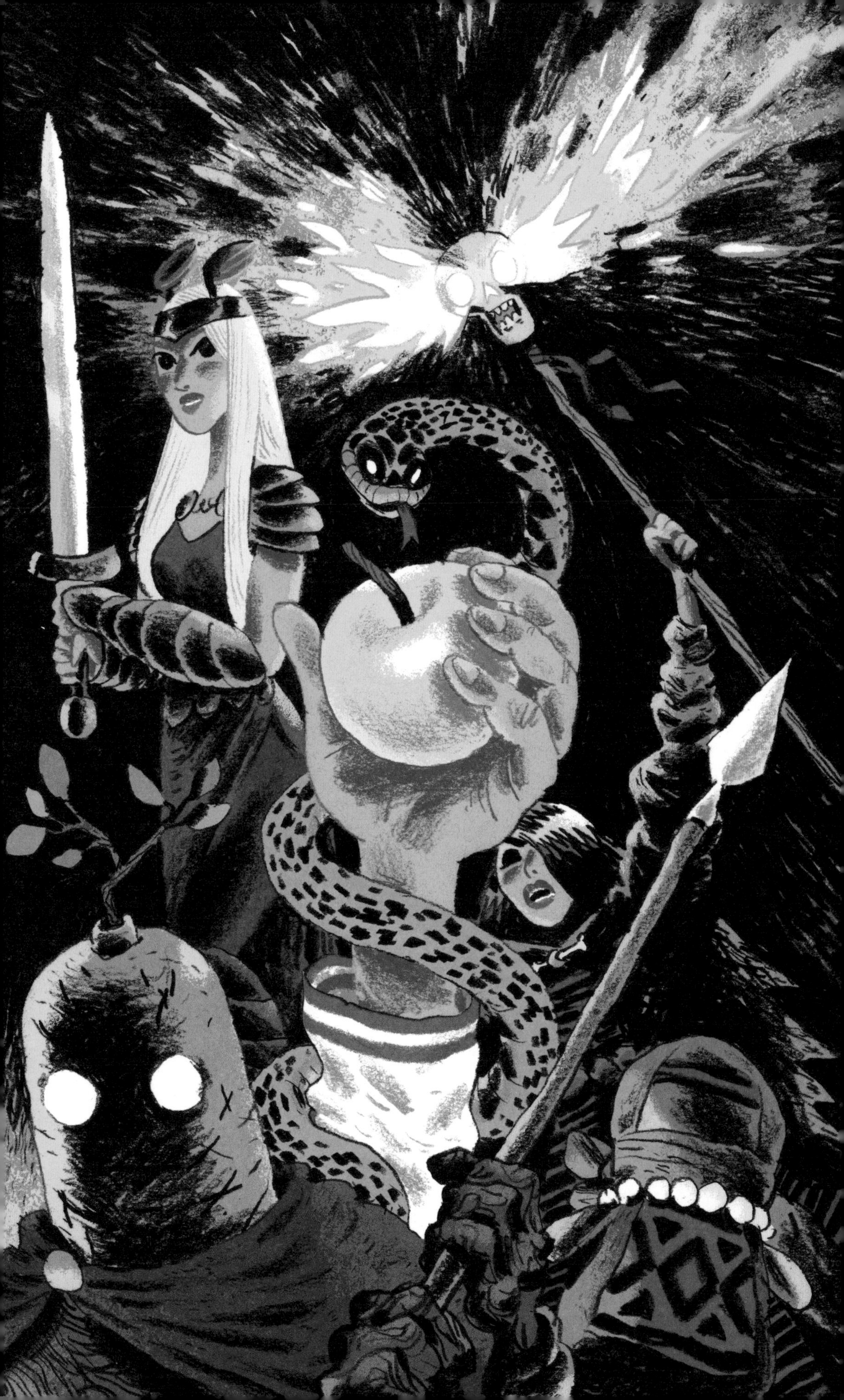

READ MORE TALES FROM THE GRIPPING SERIES:

GAMAYUN TALES
THE KING OF BIRDS
ALEXANDER UTKIN
NOBROW

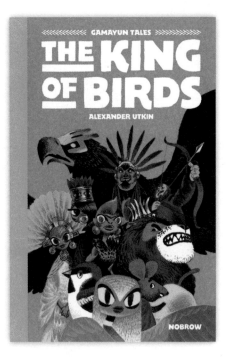

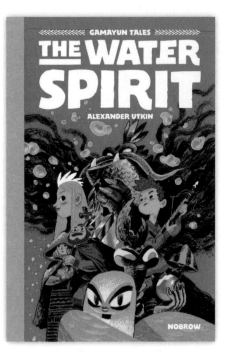

IBSN: 978-1-910620-38-0

GAMAYUN TALES
THE WATER SPIRIT
ALEXANDER UTKIN
NOBROW

IBSN: 978-1-910620-48-9

FIRST EDITION PUBLISHED IN 2019 BY NOBROW LTD.
27 WESTGATE STREET, LONDON E8 3RL.

TRANSLATION BY LADA MOROZOVA.

3 5 7 9 10 8 6 4 2

PUBLISHED IN THE US BY NOBROW (US) INC.

PRINTED IN LATVIA ON FSC® CERTIFIED PAPER.

MIX
Paper from responsible sources
FSC® C002795
FSC www.fsc.org

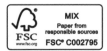

ISBN: 978-1-910620-51-9

WWW.NOBROW.NET